AUXILIARY
# SKINS

T0096254

# AUXILIARY
# SKINS

A Collection of Stories

CHRISTINE MISCIONE

Library and Archives Canada Cataloguing in Publication

Miscione, Christine, 1986-, author
    Auxiliary skins : a collection of stories / Christine Miscione.

ISBN 978-1-55096--353-3 (pbk.)

    I. Title

PS8626.I81A89 2013          C813'.6          C2013-902877-3

Design and Composition by Mishi Uroboros
Cover Art by Luke Siemens
Typeset in Fairfield, Trajan and Constantia fonts at Moons of Jupiter Studios

Published by Exile Editions Ltd ~ www.ExileEditions.com
144483 Southgate Road 14 – GD, Holstein, Ontario, N0G 2A0
Printed and Bound in Canada in 2013, by Imprimerie Gauvin

We gratefully acknowledge, for their support toward our publishing activities, the Canada Council for the Arts, the Government of Canada through the Canada Book Fund (CBF), the Ontario Arts Council, and the Ontario Media Development Corporation.

The use of any part of this publication, reproduced, transmitted in any form or by any means, electronic, mechanical, photocopying, recording, or otherwise stored in a retrieval system, without the expressed written consent of the publisher (info@ exileeditions.com) is an infringement of the copyright law. For photocopy and/or other reproductive copying, a license from Access Copyright (800 893 5777) must be obtained.

Canadian Sales: The Canadian Manda Group, 165 Dufferin Street, Toronto ON  M6K 3H6    www.mandagroup.com    416 516 0911

North American and International Distribution, and U.S. Sales:
Independent Publishers Group, 814 North Franklin Street,
Chicago IL  60610    www.ipgbook.com    toll free: 1 800 888 4741

*For Nicholas*

# Skin, Just

Gum on the sidewalk, and all she can see are moles misshaped, moles deadly. Layers of tar covering potholes are moles too, tar on every street, melanoma in every city. And polka-dot bathing suits. And specks on shower tiles. Knots on floorboards, bruises on banana skins, rot in apples, soy sauce drips left over on tables and the arms of strangers, their tank-topped backs, their miniskirted legs where skin shines through: moleless, moleful, abnormal, normal, happy.

Happy Moles is the name of a band she imagined starting with her next-door neighbour Petey and his younger sister Tessa. The three of them could take photos of their moles and magnify them on T-shirts. Wear them to every gig. Sell some after the show with their signatures underneath: *Wear our moles with pride*. Except Tessa didn't have any moles. She was clear as a cup of water. She was so see-through you could see through to her veins, her bones, joints oiled and colon cancer screening made easy.

*Patient demands assistance immediately, wants biopsy of mole. Mole approximately five millimetres, but hard to discern. Sample covered in blood.*

It was growing down there for a long time. She saw it day after day, and the colour became angry. At first it was only a little baby speck, full of exuberance, ready for life. These were the happy days, when Happy Moles, the band, was a possibility. But then: slowly, itty bitty slowly, itty bitty baby mole began to get greedy. Wanted fame. Wanted to rock the calf right out of an auditorium with hundreds of screaming fans—

But it wasn't to be.

And then ANGER. Crawling anger. Anger slowly turning to multifarious shades of dark. Mole becoming monochrome. Sullen. Mole brooding in its epidermal throne, sinking lower and lower into layers of flesh, lower into dermis, then hypodermis where it grew manic and uncontrollable.

The growing wouldn't stop.

Wild aberrations, crazed mounds of melanocytes in skin's pigmental, skin overfloweth, her cup overflowing with showers of melanoma sparkles. All dangerous hues. All mutations in sacs of jelly mounds of mole on her calf and chest and down to the base of her spine where moles congregated to praise our Lord Jesus Christ, save her. Save her.

But sadly nothing could be saved. Not an inch or a centimetre. Not the skin protecting, skin holding in. Not the layers of billowy cauliflower florets bulbous in her brain, where thoughts began, where meat was turned to neuronal passages long ago during Neanderthal times. This is evolution: blue eyes. Fair skin. Deranged cells. Abysmal passages in neuroland. This is evolution: Skin cells replicating infinity. Skin cells never stopping. Skin cells' immortal magic.

Until one day she couldn't take it anymore. Squatting in her bedroom. Staring at her calf, at her mole growing crazy – SHE COULD NOT TAKE IT ANYMORE. How much can be encapsulated in that phrase? She, a pronoun. Could, separated from Not. Could, Not. Could, a verb of possibility. Not, the destroyer. Not destroys Could's possibility, as though errant pigment destroys She. Or Her. Take, a verb. It, a pronoun. Anymore, a state of being. Wrapped together: a phrase leading to action, leads to slicing open skin and digging out the darkness.

Because she just couldn't take it anymore. On her calf. She could not take it anymore on her calf, so she knifed it out of there. Dug like an excavation. Messy like a construction site. Blood everywhere like menstruation, and she just couldn't take it anymore, so she rushed to the doctor's. Demanded care.

Demanded more action. "Doctor, Doctor, here's my mole. Look at my mole. Examine my mole, NOW! I have cancer. I have cancer in my mole and I need treatment immediately."

*Patient presents with calf mole. Mole is cut out and in her hand.*

It was the gasoline spill on the pavement outside her house. It was the way gasoline turns normal tar dark and irregular. It was how Tessa's molelessness destroyed Happy Moles, made her own skin seem speckled and malignant, made everything cancerous, cancer-filled, moles full of cancer. It was the way the ROM sprouted its own side growth, its jagged tumour, darkly pigmented zigzag malignancy sticking right out the fucking top and down the side while she was walking Bloor St. and couldn't take it anymore.

*Patient slips in and out of consciousness. Post-traumatic stress and blood loss from "biopsy." Patient refuses treatment and sedatives. Patient wants mole tested.*

And then mole from calf in hand, mole in hand in front of doctor. Doctor takes mole into hands, puts mole in bag. Doctor packages mole for laboratorial assessment.

*Patient's mole sent to laboratory. Advised patient to seek emergency counselling and take sedatives. Patient refused. Will return when results are received.*

And then waiting. Long stretch of waiting. Days and weeks of waiting. Heaving in her upstairs bedroom, hyperventilating. Reaching internet limits of skin cancer research. Scouring website after website, and then back to the beginning, first website first, then return to the second. Every day the same cyber circuit, the same heaving in her upstairs bedroom. And she doesn't eat. She doesn't sleep. Fungus grows on food: pancake tumours, floret moulds. Fungus grows on her mole-hole, infection everywhere, and she can't bear to look at it. She refuses. And now a big open sore fringed with pus. And now a hole where a mole used to be. And she's waiting, moulding and waiting, moulding and waiting—

Until one day it comes.

A twinkling ring. A call from a receptionist. A soft-spoken charm through the phone earpiece: "Come in immediately, Dr. Urbanstein wants to see you. Your test results are in."

And then such *hurry hurry*. Dirty clothes thrown over dirty body, thrown into a taxicab speeding down College St., "Hurry, please, HURRY… Can't you go a little faster? I really have to get there NOW" – And jeans rub against calf-hole, rubbing dirty bacteria into calf-hole while taxicab swerves around cars, flies forward, quick left, left again, hands gripping seat cushion near calf-hole, hole leaky, bacterial, hole thrown left and right, cab turns, turns again and comes to a stop. Then: a money exchange. A door slam. The *tap tap tap* of feet hurrying across concrete, feet into a doorway.

"Clara Williamson...Yes, here to see Dr. Urbanstein. Yes, I received a call this morning... OK, thank you."

Feet tapping in a waiting room is not so unusual. Every patient taps something, fiddles something else, picks at other things while anxiously awaiting his or her turn. Flipping through sticky magazines isn't so unusual either – pick off crumbs on page seventeen, look at celebrity photos on page twenty-two, skim facts about silk-lined pillowcases and titillating meatloaf. But leaking holes on carpeted ground in a waiting room is irregular. Taxicab excitement tore it open again, blood dripping into jean fabric, and now it trickle-trickles on the floor.

OK, OK, so she's got an open wound. OK, so it's leaking everywhere, staining, stinking, but at least her results are in. At least she can be told what she could not know about her own body. At least the doctor can put it all on the table and tell her how much longer she has to live.

*Patient looks skeletal, infection in her right calf where seven-millimetre mutilation occurred. Antibiotics prescribed. Patient self-describes as anxious and psychotic. Confirms she has not eaten in at least six days.*

Cut to the chase, Doctor. She's not here to talk about her health. She doesn't care about infection. She doesn't want your antibacterials, your food suggestions, your sedation medications to relieve the stress of sitting here waiting for you to tell her the fucking results. Just give them to her. Tell her what her skin cells said. Tell her how much longer. Tell her what her mole was!

Negative.

Test results are negative; skin pigments are negating cancerous undertones, negating intra-body travel to different regions for fun in the sun and relaxation. But that can't be possible! – Can that be possible? Is it possible for skin cells, angry and black, to be jolly jubilee? Did she cut her mole, defile her calf, let infection seep for eight days all for NOTHING?

*Patient seems upset at results. Patient bangs hand on forehead continuously. Eventually forced hand onto her lap. Appears patient has violence and anger management issues. Prescribed several medications listed below and six days of antibiotics to clear infection. Patient is discharged from clinic.*

Tight grip on her antibacterial prescription. Fingers clasping antipsychotics, anti-anxieties, sedatives, sleeping pills. Five slips of prescriptions in her hand, she marches out of the doctor's office, out onto the concrete, into the sun, sun burning her eyelids, and there's a wrenching pain in her gut, fingers twisting her spleen and stomach into happy organ animals, insides burning like eyelids. All for nothing. All for nothing! Body RUINED all for nothing.

Then: five days of antibiotics, pus slurps back to origin, blood crusts into a convex dome, blackens, misshapes. Every day her mantra: ALL FOR NOTHING. Five days of nausea, puke in the bathroom, the kitchen, lethargy on her bed. She can barely get up. Antibiotics suck the life force out of people. But she wouldn't move anyway, even if she felt perfectly fine, even if the doctor assured her she'd live for another forty years. Because she can't bear to look in the mirror and face herself, what she did, how she self-mutilated for no particular reason. Wasn't cancer. Not melanoma. Not basilique or squirmish.

And, sure, the mole-hole starts to heal. No more infection or open wound. Instead: a concave dip, right where the dig happened. An irreversible hole where her mole used to be. And, sure, she's healthy, cancer-free, should be rejoicing, should be out dancing in the streets, living life again…

But all she can do is sit on her bed. Her calf-dip killing her. She can't take it, just can't bear to look at it, and everywhere – EVERYWHERE – holes dip, acne pits, the dip in the sidewalk outside her house, the blemishes of Christie Pits. She throws herself onto her bed and imagines the multitudes of dips and pits that surround her, doesn't want to face the world. Moves inward, into the centre, begins to fetal curl, but her bed dips. And her pillow dips. And she slams her fist onto the mattress making an itty-bitty pit. She just can't escape the pits and dips, the highs and lows. She just can't hide from holes and concavity. Moles and convexity. Skin is everywhere, surfaces everywhere, surfaces and skins ready to dip and valley, pit and dale, normal, abnormal, happy. And so it goes. She sighs, curls inward, fetal curl until she's nothing but a ball. A mole. A small growth of otherwise benign skin.

# BREACHED HEREDITY

It was the anniversary of my sister's twelfth birthday and five days till Easter. Pepé didn't know what kind of cake to order but he liked the idea of purple sugar balloons. Apparently even in sadness we could be elated.

Pepé is the biggest Latino I know and he just so happens to be married to Ma. Ma looks Latino too but can't speak a damn word of Spanish. She hangs off Pepé's arm and lets him do all the español while I sit in the background and watch.

I sigh and Pepé tells me all sorts of philosophical bullshit about my sister's spirit still being alive in the "gardens of the mortality" or so he calls it. He says to celebrate her birth is to resurrect and settle her death. He's always talking about the afterworld and other sentimental shit. Thinks he's real deep. He doesn't understand that on the anniversary of my sister's twelfth birthday all I want to do is mourn her passing. She's dead. And no purple frosting or sugar balloons will bring her back.

Pepé loses hope. He looks crushed. He pushes the Build-a-Cake flyer across the table towards Ma: "I would just like to help, no?" His defence for everything. Pepé does what he wants then claims he's helping us, like we're unlucky half-breeds, two mutts living in Canada. And sometimes, maybe we are.

Don't get me wrong, I like Pepé. He's a man and I haven't had one in the house for years. My other father was one of those guys with big rippling muscles and his chest hair shaved off. He fathered my sister too, and look how that turned out.

Thinking of those early years makes me real thankful for Pepé. Why wouldn't I be? My other father would come crashing through my bedroom door. He'd yell for me to go right there in front of him. Afterwards I'd hear Ma screaming from her bedroom. She locked herself inside. She was trying to stay alive, and all I could hear was her small scared voice, "Tatty, Tatty, please run away! RUN AWAY! Tatty!"

I remember after fights like that she'd always bring him back to their bedroom, lock the door, and I'd hear them fucking all night. Monsters don't only live in closets or under beds. Ma chose to ignore that, then Joycie came along, and now fifteen years later we can't decide what to celebrate.

Pepé brushes his long hair aside and tries again, "*Please*, celebration is good for both of you, no?"

He's just trying to help and sometimes I want to pinch his soft Latino cheeks and say thank you. But usually I just want to rip them from his face and glue them onto mine so maybe I'd belong somewhere.

I get up from the table and cross the kitchen to hug Ma. She looks real confused. Missing Joycie probably or maybe stressed because Easter is in a few days. I sometimes wonder if it's hard for her to be around me knowing I came from him too. I could've ended up the same way.

"Baby's kicking a whole lot, Ma. Here, feel it."

I put her hand on my belly. She opens her mouth but nothing comes out.

❦❦❦

Back when Pepé was thirty his parents died and left him nothing. Apparently his father owned a big business in South America years ago and Pepé's whole life there was luxury and fun. But now Pepé has inherited nothing except debt. He's a moving man Monday to Friday. *Carlos Marquez Movers.* He isn't muscular like my other father but real agile. His hands are callused too, just the way I like them down my back, rough and tickly. Sometimes he looks more like a friendly rat than a human to me, especially when he's happy after an orgasm. And his body always feels like a shaggy carpet when I touch it, hair all over the place. I wonder if Ma thinks so too.

***

Yesterday afternoon Pepé spewed out some philosophical bullshit about spilling juice all over his bedsheets after I tumbled from them. My round belly nearly touched down on the hard wooden floor below the bed, but Pepé saved me. He said something about catching the horse before it blew open and really he meant not having my uterus smash apart with bits of fetus all over the floor. He didn't want to mess up our dirty sex-sheets any more than they already were so that if Ma came home she wouldn't know.

"Don't you think she'll find out anyway, huh? The baby is due in a month!"

Pepé helped me up from the floor then to my bedroom. He told me that we shouldn't be fucking so close to the due date. I said, "I don't give a shit so long as Ma doesn't find out." Which meant, kill the baby with your prick, see if I care. And besides, don't tell me this after we've just fucked. Get your fun and then be the responsible parent? Makes me sick but then I felt sick anyway.

When my hormones are level and I'm not pregnant, us together, it's nothing like that. It's not sick. We're not. In fact, when I'm with Pepé it's because I want to be. His arms around my body make me feel protected. He plays with my hair too. It's just, sometimes he can't help himself and pretends like I've got nothing inside me, like I'm not pregnant. He goes rough in me then calls me a freak. He tells me to get out of his room. Dinner after is real awkward. Ma'll serve us mashed potatoes and we can't even look at each other.

ᘜᘜᘜ

Ma works hard at the grocery store. She's worked her way up to bakery manager and I'm real proud of her efforts. Pepé says something like, "The mountains are hard to surpass, but she's on the other side." Pepé says I should appreciate the mountains that surround us, but I don't think so. Calgary is a sore place. Nothing happens here. I ran away to Vancouver once. I was fourteen years old and lived on the street for two weeks. I was with a friend so it was okay. It actually turned out to be more of a party than anything else because we'd sneak into clubs and meet guys, go home with them and let them fuck us for a warm place to stay. I never told Ma any of this because it'd break her heart. She'd think it was all her fault and I never want her thinking that. Pepé doesn't know either. I want to tell him that if it weren't for him I would've ended up there permanently.

❦❦❦

Ma thinks I'm a lush but I say, "I wasn't born liking scotch, Ma, only after Joycie died."

I'm fine though. I've only had two drinks since I found out about the baby. Two. That's pretty good and both those times I had to. The first was on my twentieth birthday, seven months ago. My other father tried calling me. I hadn't heard from that scum for years and all of a sudden he had the nerve to call? Well, Pepé picked up the phone, found out who it was and started screaming at him. I ran out of the house crying and don't remember the rest of the evening.

The second drink I had was because I was upset too. All I remember was I came home from work and heard Pepé and Ma fucking upstairs. It was the loudest sex I ever heard and Pepé kept telling her how much he loved her. He never says that to me.

When I think about it I feel like Judas being used by God. Because that's what I thought of when the priest told us the Easter story today. It's Good Friday and I thought of how Jesus and God needed Judas to betray them so their little Easter plan would work out. They used him and made him do it the same way Pepé uses me now. But he's the father of my child and I love him, what am I supposed to do.

❧❧❧

Ma says if I'm pregnant I shouldn't have a single drop of alcohol because the baby will turn to mush. She says she had a friend once who was a heavy drinker and drank all through the pregnancy and what popped out after nine months wasn't even human. I said, "Ma, aren't you talking about yourself?"

Pepé stays quiet through these discussions because he knows I shouldn't be pregnant in the first place. Sometimes he says I'm not and it's all in my head. Then Ma tells him to shut up and let me be. "She's fragile."

❧❧❧

My big belly reminds me a lot of the Easter eggs I want to paint but also bloating and constipation. I used to have it real bad. It started the last few times my other father came into my bedroom. I remember my glow-in-the-dark stars on the ceiling and so many stuffed animals around me and his big muscles showing. He grabbed my hair. He forced my pants off.

Nothing came out.

I'd never seen him as angry as the first time my body wouldn't listen. Afterwards I was constipated for a year pretty much. My belly swelled but Ma was too busy trying to get over Joycie. I never told her about it back then. If she had looked though, she would've seen I was just a big dome of shit the same way I am now except now I'm one month till my due date.

⦉⦊⦉⦊⦉⦊

I wonder what Ma'll say when baby pops out a fucking collage of everyone it's related to. It'll be like me. Nowhere. But I'm hoping it'll look more like Pepé and speak Spanish. I'd like that and then maybe I can be somewhere too.

My boss at the gas station gave us Good Friday and Easter Monday off which is unusual and nice but Pepé says it's the way it should be. "No one should have to work on Jesus Christ's Easter day." Pepé wouldn't even fuck me on Good Friday. He says it's sacrilegious. He looked at me blankly yesterday afternoon when I put my hand on his dick and rubbed.

I'm happy to have the whole weekend off but I feel like I'm carrying a pile of soggy laundry under my shirt. I feel burdened or something. I want to rip it from under there or sit on the toilet and let it out. Today I asked Pepé if he still found me attractive. He put his hand on my shoulder and told me nothing has changed. I'm still the same person I always was.

❧❧❧

It's Easter Sunday but our big Easter dinner is coming up tomorrow. We're having Aunt Cindy and Uncle Rick over, their kids, and Pepé's sister from Toronto. Ma asked me to decorate some eggs after lunch so I did. I made them pretty with different swirls of colour. My Easter eggs don't look anything like eggs anymore but like little drops of daydream. I'll tell Pepé this later and see what he says.

Afterwards I set my painted eggs in a basket in the family room and overheard Ma and Pepé talking. They were talking about me and the baby, saying things I couldn't really hear. So I barged in there and demanded they say it straight to my face. I don't know what came over me. I hate when people talk about other people behind their back like that, especially after what happened to Joycie.

They both looked at me and Ma seemed real sad. "Oh, Tatty. Don't ruin Easter over this, okay? Your due date will come around and you'll know what we mean." But I still have one month so that's no use. I don't care what they were saying anyway. Pepé was probably saying I don't have a baby in me because he doesn't want Ma to know. He's a liar and can't keep his dick in his pants. Sometimes I wish we never started fucking three years ago or that Ma never married him.

CCC

Easter Monday is turning into a real letdown. My belly ached for a few hours this morning but as soon as I threw up I felt better. Ma went shopping for some vegetables while Pepé and I made out in the bathroom. He just had a shower so it was real steamy in there. It reminded me of a tropical rainforest and Pepé's life in Argentina. He promised to take me down there one day but when I reminded him about it today he said I need to get better first. I asked him if that's what he thought of his child, a sickness or some disease that I need to get better from. He shook his head and said, "Look at yourself,

Tatty." Then he left me with my legs spread apart on the wet tiles. I thought: This baby better pop out soon because Pepé won't even fuck me anymore.

Afterwards I waddled back to my bedroom so I could die under my sheets until Ma came home. She'd know what to say to make it better. She'd kiss me on the cheek or rub my head or something. But when Ma came to me she seemed real distant. She had that same crooked smile on her face that she had when we found Joycie. I said, "Ma, why are you looking at me like that?" She shook her head. I said again, "Ma, why are you looking at me like that? Stop it." But she wouldn't. She just sat on the wooden chair by my bed and stared at me. Not even sad, just crooked and distant. I tried to roll over on my side but my belly was too fat. I didn't want to hurt the baby. I asked her to come help me and said it nicely too, "Ma, can you please come help me roll over?" All she said was, "I found a condom on the bathroom floor, Tatty. A half-opened wrapper with a condom hanging out near Pepé's pants. Did you leave that there?"

❦❦❦

Pepé swears we always used condoms to fuck. I say, "Then how the hell can I be pregnant?" We're sitting at the kitchen table while the lamb is roasting and Ma keeps screaming for me to shut up. "Stop talking about that goddamn baby, Tatty! I can't hear another word about it!" But what am I supposed to do? Just ignore that it's inside me? It kicks and I shudder. I feel bloated and want to burp it out but nothing works. And soon the guests are coming.

Ma's vegetables are boiling over and I watch her walk to the stove. She stands there for a while. I can hear her crying. Then I look over at Pepé and all he's doing is staring at the ground. I say, "What are you so sulky about?" Ma tells me to shut up again then goes up to her bedroom.

From the kitchen table I can see my Easter eggs in the family room painted so pretty. What would it be like to be Ukrainian? I've always wanted to know ever since I learned they were the ones who invented egg painting. Maybe they were pregnant too and wanted everyone to celebrate with them. Easter is the one time when the whole world has eggs and new things are born, just like Jesus. This year it's five days after the anniversary of my sister's twelfth birthday and one month until my due date. Time flies real fast. After dinner I tell Ma I'm so full I'm about to burst. She says, "Yeah, you're definitely full of something."

# Roidal Conundrum

Topic: swollen inj site, maybe infection?

**Joe289 –**

Sun, 2010-09-19 12:15

I homebrewed some yesterday in the a.m, high BA and this wasn't junk. Inj with 23g 1/2 pin and it burned like a mother. didn't expect it to. bicep started to get patchy with red bits and some kind of purplish circle around the inj site. Today my hole is pusy as fuck can't even see where pin went in. and delt is swollen up. Not hard, when I poke my finger in it its really soft like jello. Has anyone had this before? ANY HELP GREATLY APPRECIATED

**Dr. Meeple2230 –**

Sun, 2010-09-19 16:15

yeah bro, see tha doctor asap. Maybe the pin wasn't fresh? You need to disinfect INJ site too. I always do anyway.

**Petra —**

Sun, 2010-09-19 16:45

I had something like two years ago...... I injected with 33g dental needle in left quad... Don't ask where I got it! lol, but it didn't do n e thing for me.... sounds like I had the exact same infection as you...... And I seen a friend of mine go through the same thing. Doctor stuck an antibiotic prick in her ass... she couldn't sit for the rest of the day! ... lol ... my infection cleared w/o doc. Plus I have no insurance so I guess I had to suck it up lol

**Joe289 —**

Sun, 2010-09-19 17:00

@ Dr. Meeple2230.... Have you had this type of thing before? I used those alcohol pads and a fresh needle (obviously). It's been over 24hrs now and the delt is bigger then ever. don't know what to do because it hurts like hell and I don't have insurance too. Today is me and my girlfriend's two year anniversary and I don't think i can go out like this in public. none of my shirts fit over that delt unless I stretch really hard, but then I'll ruin the shirt! and all this fluid is like collecting further down in the bicep. doesn't look good.

**IronMan007 –**

Sun, 2010-09-19 20:19

DON'T BE A PUSSY. TAKE YOUR FUCKING GIRL OUT FOR A GOOD DINNER. STERIODS DON'T MAKE YOU A MAN BUT YOUR ACTIONS DO. SUCK IT UP BITCH.

*Life is what you make it.*

*—Chinese Proverb*

**Dr. Meeple2230 –**

Sun, 2010-09-19 22:43

nop never had that before sorry bro.

**SexyLacy –**

Sun, 2010-09-19 22:47

ANYONE WANNA HAVE SOME REAL XXX FUN? Sexy girlz looking for a someone big and hard like youuuuu

**SteelTiger –**

Sun, 2010-09-19 23:22

No doubt you *must* see a doctor, friend. Though I've come to despise them over the years. I know you don't have insurance, but would you rather die? Infections can become septic in a matter of minutes. I watched a dear love one die infamously from an infected appendix that spread systemically. And we don't even need the appendix.

## Joe289 –

Sun, 2010-09-19 23:57

@SteelTiger. ....your right. Just moneys a bit tight right now. Trying to save up for better homebrew kit and stuff. But your right i should go. I don't want to die.

❦❦❦

## Joe289 –

Mon, 2010-09-20 8:24

Day two and arm still swollen like a motherfucker. can't seem to push fluid anywhere it just sits there. And pus is turning a blue colour, like really sick blue with green bits around the outside. nasty stuff. INJ completely covered in it thinking maybe its some kind of chemical reaction? I'm confused because I know I did everything right. gf is mad because i ditched her last night, but I couldn't explain everything that's going on. She doesn't know i'm juicing and I can't tell her.

## Joe289 —

Mon, 2010-09-20 9:43

I sound like such a pussy on here but seriously bros not sure what to do. Can't get into see a doctor I have no cash. My friend's friend is a nurse so maybe can see her but at this point I don't think I can even leave my apt. arm is like a blimp and veins ggoing to INJ site are turning black.

## Dr. Meeple2230 —

Mon, 2010-09-20 13:58

dude, see a doctor, go to emerg. this isnt normal pip

## Joe289 —

Mon, 2010-09-20 14:07

@Dr. Meeple2230… I want to see a doctor but I'm really low on cash right now. Like no money. This could easily cost me over $1000 I think. My parents don't give a shit about me since I started juicing it and if I asked them for money they'd think I was using to buy more gear. My gf Lisa is annoyed too she won't even answer my phone calls and I can't exactly go over to her apt. I'm in a really big mess right now and think I may have to just go into emerg like you said but it looks impossible right now.

**Joe289 –**

Mon, 2010-09-20 16:42

Right now veins are blacker then before. all of the veins going into INJ site and around the pus patch, really black. arm filling with more liquid now it's near my hands and becoming hard to type this. ANY ADVICE?

**Joe289 –**

Mon, 2010-09-20 17:02

Anyone out there today?

**Joe289 –**

Mon, 2010-09-20 18:36

Reallu considering going to emerg. Bicep and delt basically nonexistent and no definition just jello. tried putting a shirt on just now but it won't fit over and hurt like hell to force it. Gf wants to come over and I'm not sure what to do???? Arm veins blacker then ever seen them, looks like my arm is DYING.

**Joe289 –**

Mon, 2010-09-20 20:29

Still sitting here basically watching my arm die. can't put on any clothes and have no appetite. confused and angry that this even happened when I FOLLOWED ALL THE INSTRUCTIONS VERY CAREFULLY. in too much pain to punch the wall or else I would. I have to keep putting kleenx on the pus to keep it from dripping all over my keyboard.

※※※

**Blasphemous_Buck –**

Tues, 2010-09-21 01:16

R.I.P Joe289's Arm. May it Rot In HELL…..
hahaha……………

**Joe289 –**

Tues, 2010-09-21 01:23

@ Blasphemous_Buck… fuck you, man, this isn't funny you prick. Can't sleep worth shit. I want to but it hurts too much. I read somewhere online that I gotta keep the arm elevated. Trying but there's no strength in my delt or any of the muscles on that side. Anyone know what to do?

**Ned.Loves.Cleo.1986 –**

Tues, 2010-09-21 03:17

Oh, yes, I've had this! Elevation = good. But better = sawing off the bad parts and putting them in the fridge. I've heard that electromagnetic energy and coolants work wonders for infectious and inflammation of the muscle. Have you ever thought of lobotomy? It helped me.

**Joe289 –**

Tues, 2010-09-21 03:36

@Ned.Loves.Cleo….. No, never heard of putting my arm in the fridge or anything. Ive been seeing online that if I crush up some aspirin and add water to make this kind of serum liquid I can inj that in and it will help. Have you had experience with this?

**Ned.Loves.Cleo.1986 –**

Tues, 2010-09-21 04:17

Yes.

**Joe289 –**

Tues, 2010-09-21 04:44

Did it work?

**Joe289** –

Tues, 2010-09-21 06:08

Did it work???

**Joe289** –

Tues, 2010-09-21 09:02

Hello??????????????????????

**SexyLacy** –

Tues, 2010-09-21 10:27

ANYONE WANNA HAVE SOME REAL XXX
FUN? Sexy girlz looking for a someone big and hard
like youuuuu

**Joe289** –

Tues, 2010-09-21 11:02

fuck it I'm going to try it.

**Joe289** –

Tues, 2010-09-21 13:01

INJected six dissollved aspirin w two tablespoons
of baking soda in my delt muscle near puss area.
Fucking hurt to poke into arm no blood came up but

this yellow fluid stuff did. It stank. Veins in my arm and shoulder still black as hell. both hands becoming shaking and my tongue feels numb too? Pain is still there but not really because it feels more like a numb pain if thats possiblle. Really shaky as i type this too not sure whats going on.

◖◖◖

**cribs –**

Fri, 2012-04-13 11:17

Hey Guys! I know it's be like two years since you guys posted about this, but recently I got the same thing in my bicep musc. I'm staring at it right now and it looks red, almost like my son's fire truck. It hurts a shitload. I only want to go to the doctor's if I have to. I'm wondering @Joe289 – did you end up going to the drs? If so what did he say and did it cost a lot for any treatments? I have some insurance but my dr doesn't know I'm using roids.

Thx.

# TIMOROUS IN LOVE

Beautiful man. Beautiful scarf-wearing man. Man under duress, dressed up in a baby blue scarf and studded cowboy boots. Boots up to his knees crossed, and hands on knees are clammy, and hands wear chunky jewels bejewelling clamminess because he's shy. And he's a thinking man, a singing man, a singer-songwriter-soulful man, performing under duress of his dress and audience stares. My favourite song: "Cleavage of Persona and Person." The lyrics leave his mouth travelling room to ears, entering ears to canals, and words in canals are brilliant, and words wax too abstract to understand. But he's singing about shyness. Debilitating shyness. His own shyness, because he's a shy man. And he's defining shyness in one hundred ears. He's saying shyness is fullness, need-an-audience fullness, and *I'm shy*, he says, filling one hundred ears.

Then in leopard-print pants the next day. Feathered scarf the next day. He's a shy man with defined eyebrows. He's a yellow-pleather-purse man. A heartbreaker. A singer. He's bashful in frilly leotard. Timorous in red lipstick. A man of lace gloves that hold hands with a man in suspenders, and all four hands stroking later in positions For Men Only, on bed sheets For Men Only, with twists and thrusts For Men Only, no women allowed. And what shyness as he struts, his pleather dangling, and the click-clicks of studded cowboy boots. And what fullness as he writes songs that sparkle, with pens that shine, pens writing songs about men and love and shyness, and his work is exalted, and his work is profound, and he's a superstar of a man, a super-extraordinary man, a man like no other around.

And no one knows what it's like to see his shy brow furrow above blue eye-shadow's creasing, as timid blush glitters beside his pink mouth that's speaking. Because he's speaking about love. And he's singing about shyness. And his lip curls to smile, and eyes soften in kindness. And no one knows what it's like to write him an email later, "Ode to a Beautiful Scarf-Wearing Man." Then every day by your computer, fingers clicking beside your computer, mouse scrolling, neck cramping, eyes glazing beside your computer. And every day moving in and out of an email inbox. Waiting in front of an email inbox. Hoping and waiting for a reply, a *Bonjour*, for something, anything in an email inbox from the beautiful scarf-wearing man.

But nothing ever comes.

Instead you watch him in dimly lit taverns. His jade beret bashful. His pink halter shining. He struts and he laughs and spills brilliance in *other* ears, his smile filling *other* eyes, while you're invisible in dark corners, a ghost, a groupie. No one knows what can happen to your heart when your heart sits in an email inbox, ignored. When your heart loves a man of scarves, a shy man, a man nothing like his shyness, who instead clicks his high heels across tavern stages, *click-click-clicking* into ear canals, and dive-bar laughter, and later, *click-clicks* under bed sheets, filling holes in bed with another man.

No one knows how it feels to fill your own bed with straight men. To kiss and fuck straight men. Filler for your hole, because you're not a man yourself. And to always kiss perfect strangers. To floss and smell perfect strangers. Floss your left molar and smell Tommy. In-between canine and incisor, Jake. And bits of Christopher fling onto your bathroom mirror four days after you kissed him because you only floss once a week, and you kiss a lot of men, and all the men you kiss, you kiss to replace the one who has your heart in his email inbox, the beautiful scarf-wearing inbox, ·the man of shyness and softness and pleather purses that sway.

And how your heart tumbles when he enters the bar! And your brain stops when he throws off his coat! You feel your panties rise with his eyelids – he's opening his mouth to speak: *Love and shyness* in pink lips that glitter – but you have nothing in those panties to rise. A will to rise but no manhood for hardening. No filler for filling. And you're unlovable with no penis. You're incompatible. Incongruous. Instead you're filled with everything inside of you. Full of sex and love *inside* of you. *And shyness is fullness,* a Beautiful Scarf Man once said.

And all the daydreams of gaiety with your shy man. All the fantasies of love with him, filled by him, naked together on bed sheets. And all the sleepovers in fancy pajamas. The pillow fights and giggles. Strolls with your shy man. Baths with your shy man. Bubbles and matching shower caps, lavender creams and tickles. *Oh, the kisses!* And the laughter! And all the pretty things you could do together! You'll ride buses from Hamilton to Toronto, laugh at sculptures in the AGO, pretend you're mummies in the ROM. Then you'll walk Yorkville in matching colours, dine at Bistro 990; you'll order the same thing wearing the same purple and you'll laugh together happily. And when you fall asleep at night, he'll pet your face with lace gloves because you like it. In the mornings he'll wrap you in his satin arms and kiss you, because you like it. Every Tuesday he'll loan you his leopard-print pants because you like them, and he knows that, and he wants to make you happy. Only ever wants to please you. And he'll write you words that sparkle, with pens that shine, lovely songs of whimsy and passion entwined. Then on Monday nights he'll dress in mauve tights with paisley cravat. He'll stand below your window, your beautiful shy Romeo, and profess his love to you, sing in a soprano so high your fullness will seep into panties, run down thighs.

# INTERLUDE AT NIGHT

Can't fumigate the bedroom if he's a greasy slug snoring beside me. Can't, if he's a balmy mass, a large heap producing only dank sweat to make the sheets crease lazily and stink. SUCH FILTH. There's no use wrapping myself in them, the sheets; no use in even the most innocent attempt at reclaiming sleep – falling back into it as though I climbed out voluntarily.

Enwrapped in linens I smell of him, a second layer of skin and sweat tonight and every night – repulsive. Him, a fleshy furnace sparking and misfiring; him, overheating incidentally with every effluvial reek. Was he always like this? I don't remember his yellow nails curling outward like a troll's when we first met, or his kneecaps shiny with ointments for that creeping fungus across his legs. Halitosis was the first alarm – HEY, HE'S NOT YOUNG ANYMORE – his breath curdling air in these small morning hours when I'm restless – can't sleep. I taste clotted cream in every breath with expiration dates four months ago. I inhale rot.

When I climb from that holy place of In My Dreams (where anything can happen and it does) my lungs gasp for new air – something fresh and nourishing, no decay. I remember petri dishes in grade eleven science class releasing the same odorous tumour to petrify nostrils. Decomposition 101, Revisited. And husband o' mine so devoid of respect can't allow me even one night of sleep or admit his transgression or agree to seek help, some kind of emergency counselling for nostrils to quieten up. Every morning in a daze: "Darlene, *hunny*, I can't help it... I'm *sleeping* – I don't have a clue!"

It's 2:30am, as it always is. Snores beside me are the alarm I never asked for, and with his oils shedding unabashedly it's clear: THERE WILL BE NO CEASEFIRE. So I crawl downstairs to the couch. Useless. The stench is gone, but snores rattle everywhere. Put a pillow over my ear, smells like him. Gamy candour. Spoiled flesh. See his coat strewn across the loveseat, his papers amassed on the coffee table, his slimy Kleenexes piled on the ground – feel that anger niggling in my gut, red and furious in my mind's eye – feel every inch of me covered in his skunky dandruff his sweat on me. CAN'T WIPE MYSELF CLEAN.

2:45am – the clock on the mantel – my feet dangle from the side of the couch, unsure momentarily: if there's escape, where is it?

Food during these early hours became commonplace months ago. Side-bulging love handles have grown accordingly, and feet seem to carry me from the hallway to kitchen without a thought.

2:47am – clock on the microwave – my hands open a cupboard beside the fridge revealing three platforms filled with treats. Every taste bud longing for something sensuous, STIMULATING, not in a pungent way, but simply wanting a platter of the freshest foods to smooth over damage, savour. And the whipped cream canister on the second shelf winks at me in a single sliver of light coming through kitchen windows; backyard neighbour's light must be on. I'm hazily illuminated, my finger pressing hard on the plastic nozzle swivelling cream around my tongue, frothy and distracting. More snacks? Toffee shortbread cookies? Low-sodium chips? – anything to help me forget every raw stench of him; forget his kissing-tongue, its foul longing reaching for mine in the night.

It's become devastatingly clear: the need to forget. Or to eat to distract. Then fall asleep again, wake up to something new, exciting – another life.

Chips will do. Yes, chips. And my fingers dipping in for a taste while the light coming from my neighbour's house grows diagonally through my kitchen, bounces off cupboard doors, marble countertops. I watch it grow. I eat more chips. I lick my fingers and notice two more lights flash; they dance across the lawn, spill into my kitchen windows. Seems unusual, a stray from previous nighttime indulgences when I'm pathetically alone in the dark, my eating a secret – can they see me?

Suddenly self-conscious in this light of such a large bag of chips from which I am stuffing my wrinkled mouth, my belly, faint pitiable excitement. I drop it, the bag, lick my fingers clean, then further flashes of light – and a whimper through brick padding – whimper again – something loud losing sound.

3:00am – stove clock – I edge towards the kitchen window, the frame painted cream, my ivy in curly tendrils along one side. No glasses on, I squint to make out a moving image as though a television screen, and it's Betty, the perfect neighbour, there she is, I see her curlers, her back towards me, her hand fast and rummaging through a kitchen drawer. I see a shadow in the doorway, then a man – or, it *is* a man, the shadow, a man shadow, and Betty: backyard BBQs, neighbourhood picnics, widow of three years; I water her plants every winter when she goes to Miami. Her head darts up then back to the drawer – and that man inching closer, and another sound – something guttural, unshakeable – something unlike a whimper but losing itself across our backyards.

I squint more – and shininess, metallic, long and pointed at Betty as she walks slowly backwards towards the kitchen sink, see her body suddenly halt with the cupboards, and the man, and that knife, and that's a *knife* – squinting harder – *and that's a knife!* as the knife slips inside her abdomen then up to her heart. Blood drops and Betty's back slinks down the cupboard where household cleaners are kept with the garbage bin and the dish soap and her plastic watering can I always use, and the light suddenly flashes off, then a smaller light – a flashlight? – something erratic and darting across the night. The man hurries and with the furtiveness of a shadow, looks up briefly – stares – eyes staring straight through Betty's tidy kitchen window, eyes in my gaze meeting his.

I'm ducking.

Huddling in the corner of my kitchen, chest shaking. Look up and see the abandoned bag of chips, treat cupboard still wide open, whipped cream canister forgotten. I crawl across the kitchen, down the hallway, up the stairs. I crawl through my bedroom door frame where snores overtake me again, every familiar echo in those nostrils of his, and enwrapping myself suddenly in the steady bed linens – sticky and warm – I snuggle in beside him, inhale. Everything palpable, odorous, familiar.

# WINTER IMMEMORIAL

There are three words that lately fly lazy and vacant from her lips. "I love you" feels like a circus trick, a way to get the audience to stay longer: more prattle of compliments, more kisses. She curls into an acorn, grows her shell, reaches across the bed to him and whispers, "I love you." Then silence. She's naked with linen sticky across her skin. She's clammy between thighs. And there's only silence. His grin. Sweat on his upper lip and 4:00am glaring. Tell him to leave, tell him to leave, tell him. But she pulls the blanket up to her chin, moves in closer for some tenderness, some kind of embrace. Instead, only the heartbreak of unfamiliar hands barely touching her, the *What lips my lips have kissed and where and why* – seems so foolishly romantic now, when her heart is a carnal platter, the buffet after the circus, the Four-Cunted Woman only good for a sideshow orgy. People hack her apart.

Fast-forward one week and she's curled over in a Toyota Camry, smells of rental car in the rain; all its past dredged up. Her mouth grips tighter for more friction, undulating tongue, bobbing head, his hips swerve. Fast-forward two nights and she's shotgun in a GMC Jimmy. Smells like new leather and cigarettes. He's suave, shows her the box of condoms in his glove compartment then takes her home to a stinky bachelor pad, doesn't let her take her heels off. Fast-forward five days. Her legs wide as the Grand Canyon, panting lips, sultry man's fast tongue at her, and she grabs the sheets for help. Too much flesh. Too much of *la petite mort* in the night, makes her eyes flutter, vacant. Living to die but already dead. What lips her lips have kissed and where and *why?* To repair the loneliness of I love you. To keep her pretty. To take back those nights otherwise spent alone.

❦❦❦

In the morning 8:00am is a bitter wait at the bus stop, black coffee, slush inside vinyl ankle booties and a frayed coat to her knees: faux-fur collar, no lining. It's needing cambium to regress, un-grow, go back to when she was only heartwood twig. Any time before now. Thus in the winter stands the lonely tree. Nine hours of work stretching into her future. The lines beside her mouth are cheerless and moth-eaten. 8:00am makes her thirty-six rings feel old.

At work, the usual hour after hour of gloomi-
ness. Artificial heat causes rosacea flare-ups, half
her day spent with a swollen nose. And the coughs
and sneezes of winter. The dry skin, red skin, pale
skin. The desolation of melted slush across tile
flooring, someone else's Kleenexes left behind in
the bathroom. Overhead, fluorescent lights kill any
vestige of atmosphere and beauty. Her under-eyes
are bloated, eyelids squinty, the lines on her face
appear deeper.

People come in daily with problems and misery.
They seek emergency career counselling. Her epi-
thet: *Honours B.A., Employment Counsellor*, and
she chews the end of a pen, remembers all her
clients' names, chapped skin forced into a smile
whenever they arrive. Everyone knows there's no
cure for un-saleable history. She cuts and pastes her
own Bachelor-of-Arts words into their resumes,
inserts competence. But clients are murdered in
interviews. Heads on stakes. Bloodless butchery of
every hope she incites behind the polyester of cubicle walls. They come back sobbing or "Fuck you!" or
a combination of both in some foreign slang. And
she bites her pen harder. Excuses herself to the
bathroom, dies a little more in the rickety stall, toilet flusher sweating, tampon box, smear of blood: a
momentary refuge.

After work: dollar-store pantyhose with runs up to her crotch. Slip into a new pair for dinner at Il Bar Firenze. A bottle of vino and cheap Italian food to bury three hours with an unemployed single mother, her autistic son, her twin daughters, their snot crusted on shirtsleeves, boots dripping, all stuffed into the eight-by-eight cubicle, and nothing could be done. Nothing could be done, and now saltless Tuscan bread. Mammoth slice of pizza. Heap of pasta marinara and braciole to eat away every image of that mother and her children: the four of them in a single bedroom at a women's shelter, queen bed and two cots, meals in the cafeteria, communal bathroom, shower stalls with slimy Band-Aids. Nothing could be done.

And in the winter sits the lonely tree hunched over a spread of Sicilian cannoli. She feels dizzy. Her quiet and empty boughs birdless, no song inside, no music but the jig of Italian accordion through fuzzy speakers. She finishes her pastries. Napkin. Bill. Ten minutes later it's minus twelve degrees and she's outside in the cold again, stumbles from the restaurant's icy stoop with a face full of wine, drunk half-traces. She has her apartment to look forward to – everything as she left it: darkness, heat on low, fridge empty (maybe a carton of milk, some butter), lonely sheets and blankets to slip into. But she won't go back there yet.

Eight thirty, says her watch. She's shaking on the side of the road, coat too thin, slush in her boots: a barren tree under streetlamps so desperate to avoid the chill of her economically heated apartment – so hollowed out of summer songs and the air unforgiving. She enters a phone booth, shield from the wind, dials with tremulous fingers a number she knows. A bed. A warm body next to hers. Somewhere to spread open and lose herself.

❦❦❦

February comes on like a disease. Thick phlegm is quicksand pasted across her throat. Trashcan overflowing with tissued sickness. Probably caught it from the lover who coughed all night on the other side of the bed, stuffed Kleenex in his pocket the next morning before he left. That was four days ago on the weekend. Now it's Wednesday and only half her week is gone. Days erased by sneezes and cough syrup. 6:00am alarm clock, 8:00am bus stop.

Today a doctor from Sri Lanka, newly immigrated. He slings pizza dough into perfect circles full-time. And a high-school dropout ex-convict wants to make something of his life. Another single mother. A recent university grad. A man laid off from his engineering company. Most heartbreaking: a girl, maybe fifteen, asleep in the waiting room. Find out later she was up all night with her uncle – Children's Aid had to be called. And what is desperation at fifteen? Dropping out of school to escape nightly horror? The girl says she already sold her body once; she let two grade twelve boys have sex with her from behind.

Nothing could be done, and the rest of the workday is a parade of sneezes. One after another, a runny nose, eyes irritated by the electric heat, the dust. February is unforgiving. It finds her crying in her cubicle ten minutes before work ends. She bit her pen too hard this time, syrupy blue leaks all over the sleeping girl's application form. And the girl's printing is perfect: each curve of each letter immaculately shaped, letters identical in size, so much precision. But now a nebulous blue smudge. A sticky blotch over "Date of Birth," "Employment History," "Interests." So much ink in welts across the page it's as though the fine details of the girl's life have been wiped out. All that's left to define her is the reason she wanted a job in the first place, her attempt at being set free.

When 6:00pm comes around, the night falls like a sinking elevator: slow and methodical. Reapply lipstick. Punch out on time clock. Bye to Rosie at reception. Il Bar Firenze for coffee and pizza. Bus stop. Transfer. Slink into the lordly St. George's Pub, a dive two blocks from her apartment. It always smells of vomit and musk, and she orders a gin sour, scans the room. So tired, she can't imagine the sequence of spot, stalk, seduce, fuck. Especially after a long day. And she's afraid of "I love you" falling into the night again; all that's nascent and possible sucked up a vacuum tube by those three failed words. "I love you" and she puts on a jester hat, a donkey mask. "I love you" and the winter howls through her – a long doleful cry.

But the prospect of Lonely Apartment. Envisioning herself trying to sleep alone with barging thoughts of that young girl's incest, fifteen lost forever, the rip of latex, and her own emptiness splayed across the bed. It's enough to let one-hour-later roll into the future with the wheels of a taxi: her carriage to an unknown apartment. Man at the bar, a corporate lawyer, newly divorced, his eyes far apart like a hammerhead shark. None of this matters. She kisses his neck in the taxicab, windows fog. They make out in the elevator to his apartment. Surrounded by boxes full of failed marriage, they fuck on the cool linoleum floor.

&c.&c.&c.

The rest of her work week: forty-eight hours of chapped skin, chewed pens, application forms, Il Bar Firenze, a thin coat, and minus thirteen degrees so bitter it strips bark raw. Thus the lonely tree wrapped in her worn comforter watches Seinfeld re-runs, can't sleep. Fast-forward another twenty-four hours, takes her to late Saturday night when she's draped in the sheets of an unemployed artist. One of her clients from work. The sex was short and sweet like aspartame. Fake sweetener. Something of a powdered illusion in every kiss down her neck, fingers pressing into her spine. Sweetness that fucks softly then tells her to leave before sunrise, thrusts a coat and purse in her arms. No kiss goodbye, and she staggers tipsy down a dimly lit stairwell, ploughs through EMERGENCY EXIT into the cold wintry night. Seconds later, the door alarm bursts. Sudden, unexpected shrieks. Relentless squawks so shrill and jarring they cut into the ordinariness of her evening, a serrated edge. She turns around to see what happened, then – just *walk*, keep walking, don't trip, keep going. Get the hell out of here.

By the time she hails a taxi one block down the street, the entire façade of the building is roused. Lights on in apartment windows, curious spectators, people huddled on the street to watch. The alarm

stabs through 2:30am over and over, a lunatic –
doesn't seem to be letting up any time soon. She
falls into the taxi's backseat, cold leather through
pantyhose, her stomach distended from too much
sweetener and fermenting wine. She can't fathom
the restlessness of an alarm in the night. Her exile
post-sex: idling taxi, pine-scented air freshener,
dizziness, lipstick smears, Mascara Diaspora in
racoon eyes like bruises, and she smells like him.
Sweet cologne in all the places he touched her.

Taxi tries to pull itself from the curb, but a troop
of emergency vehicles block it in. Ambulance.
Police cruisers. Fire squad. All the flashing lights
like carousel jewels, they sparkle and whirl in the
night because of her, her nose pressed up to window
glass watching. And the faintest shimmer of snow-
flakes under streetlamps, glittering moths to a star
hemmed in by darkness. Like the universe, there are
no true edges here, only moments of light across
staggering black. And those moments, blending now
into an opaque curtain pulled across taxi windows.
Policemen with intercoms, all the emergency vehicles and spectators melding together too. For a brief
minute her focus shifts to the foreground, to her
sunken face, moth-eaten, mirrored in glass – And
there, reflecting back at her through the night: a rosy
and glowing woman. An unremembered woman. A

face she used to know, sunny eyes tapping on the window glass for reply.

Two hours later, back in her apartment: nothing so disingenuous as a vaginal douching. "Cleanses history from the cave," the box claims, but not really. Instead, cans of black spray-paint covering graffiti and hieroglyphs. Layers and layers of black tar mask. Indelible ink so devoid of colour it slips into her cavernousness, her darkness – Thick concealer on the past. And what lips her lips have kissed and where and why she has forgotten. Time: A douche for the brain? The unscented irrigation of faces and little deaths, of the reek of moist underwear pulled from stranger skin? Time: So repetitious, a junkie? And where and why and where and why and where and why – all the same loaded needle. The same douche splash. Same day. Same mouth, same fuck, hack, loneliness. Same quiet pain. If she forgets it's only because there are too many to remember. Ghosts in the snow tonight – her foot high on the bathroom counter, lips apart, rubber nozzle inside. Tubes. Pump. Bag.

⚬⚬⚬

A new week. Monday morning blues and she bought herself three roses, put them on the filing

cabinet in a bevelled glass vase. Cubicle Adorn-
ments. Does it make her feel happier? The vase rat-
tles every time cabinet doors open and close. The
roses are wilting already.

Today: A defrocked priest. A relocated ESL
instructor. A woman whose left eye was fried in a
non-work-related chemical explosion wants a new
job. And a part-time journalist needs another part-
time gig. An aspiring birthday party magician wants
to supplement his dream. The usual misery behind
polyester walls.

She chews her pen, forces a smile in the sweltering artificial heat. Skin cracked and cheilitis mouth.
Under the ultraviolet radiation of fluorescent lighting, her branches are still bare. Roots still frozen and
tangled. The earth still reaching for an equilibrium
that doesn't exist.

Once 3:00pm rolls around she catches up on
filing. Has extra time, reorganizes her desk. Colour-
codes thumbtacks, paperclips, staples. Watches
the clock. It's the typical monotony of passing
hours until 6:00pm. Slip into ragged coat. Blow
nose. Reapply lipstick. Punch out on time clock.
Bye to Rosie at reception. Il Bar Firenze for heaps
of pasta marinara. Afterwards, a spread of dolci
italiani, shot of espresso. And the lonely tree, dipping a chocolate biscotti, makes eye contact with

the man three tables away. His grey hair smoothed back with gel. Five o'clock shadow. Wool scarf around his neck.

# BROKEN SWIFT

In Cootes swampland – Ontarian taste of distant Georgia – the prehistoric creatures don't enjoy company, fly away with their sewer-pipe necks, guttural sacks so large and disjointed I feel a lump in my throat watching. And their wings with gypsy fringe, their beaks shiny as sardines: the Great Blue Heron before me. Manoeuvring canoe through muck of sitting water, the parliament of bulrushes looking stately and stoic – not a breeze through them today – their density a filter for all the sludge and human waste creeping in. I watch Blue Heron take flight at the sound of my dunking paddle. I see spider lanky and elegant, long-legged fright on the bow in front of me. Up ahead, a lamentation of swans. They float across the water, thirty or more, their illusory smallness like an iceberg: each bulbous stomach hidden underwater.

I won't pretend the murkiness of swamp hasn't crawled into the mind of my friend. His dunk and pull, his paddle swish – it all feels lunatic and sticky in the turbid slime of our afternoon canoe ride. Not an inkling of wind to remind us that there's a clearing beyond the bulrushes and weeping trees – Is there a clearing? I can't remember, and the sweat on my face feels too viscid, arms heavy, feet planted; keep paddling in this soup bowl and we'll reach some kind of shore.

Rat Island.

Infestation of cormorants destroyed the ecosystem, barren and bald now, a small isle desert of birds that shit out lethal dung. Beyond the island, nothingness. Mud. Feculent runoff. We yank canoe through pebbles and excrement, invade on a cormorant colony. "What th'hell are you doing here?" some punk squawks at us; we're sitting on a shitspeckled log opening our sandwiches, hands clawing through plastic wrap. Then two others squawk a similar "fuck off!" and scurry away, dark plumage puffed and wings slightly raised.

I'm disinterested in baloney and lettuce sandwich, can only imagine inverted cups of faux-meat microwaved and sizzled. Out on the water, sun is too veiled in miasmic cloud and leafy overhang to invert me into a perfect basin for Cheese Whiz and other elementary school delicacies. We're in the smoggy haze of August. It's jungle humid here, in the verdant swampland two minutes outside and within the city. It rises discreetly from urban dirt and grime:

a hidden gem / a stagnant burden. Whichever way you want to look at it.

My half-eaten sandwich sits on the log, a pathetic hunk of Wonder Bread warped by finger imprints and saliva. Beside me, my friend looks with faraway eyes at the inferno of hot squawking cormorants that surrounds us. He stares for a while at the curtained sun. The blood of sumac. The pus of algae on sluggish water; this place is like an open sore. Then I know he's ready. He finishes my baloney and lettuce in less than ten seconds. He puts his hand on my knee. "Let's get back out there. It's time for the end" (or something like that) – all I can think about is the squish of his fingers on my skin, the way his sweat covers mine, a waxy ointment for all the future days I won't know him anymore.

On the water again. Kayaker comes into view. A hefty bovine woman from a distance, but as canoe and kayak meet, I notice thickset flab, preserved jelly under ancient Hawaiian muumuu – not so firm and oxlike as I thought. She scowls at us, screams "Fucking LOSERS!" and continues on her way through roily water.

In the swamp of Cootes Paradiso, the chorus of nature, no matter how melodious, how soulful, can be torn from you in a minute. Tarnation. Trees spontaneously defoliate, a bullet flies through your lungs. No one would be surprised. We're in Hamilton after all, a dying city. A once-Steeltown now oxidized and rusted by the murk that surrounds it from the inside, the corrosive abscess at its core. My friend loves this city, its grime and filth, its fringe of Niagaran jungle – he hopes with all his blue-collar passion that his grave will be somewhere in this swamp. I point out a sarcophagus of reeds to the left. I tell him to drown under a lily pad.

"There are more beautiful ways to die," he says.

I know what he has planned but the chubby bovine is back – "Fucking stupids! You snobby bumholes!" Her kayak looks like it's sinking slightly and I feel bad for it, cradling an ass like that, so much delusion and gas. "Fucking wimp-heads! You mama's boys!"

We're not surprised – or are we? With a quick dunk-pull of paddles in water, we try to get away but the floating beast is relentless.

"Hey, you two fucks! You stole my money! Come back here!"

A breakneck glance behind us, and I see her clumpish jowls, her psychotic mouth coming at us with a predaceous chomp. My friend and I are paddling as fast as we can, but in all the slop and sludge, we're only a few feet ahead of her. Her arms are fierce. Her arms, big-bellied like a fat man's stomach, visceral overhang, flailing abdominous. It's a chase and we have no choice but to paddle harder. We fly straight through a patch of algae, look back, and she's still on our tails. "Fucking money-snatchers! I'm going to get you!" she screams.

We round a bend. We scrape a floating log. Paddling. Paddling faster, then a swift turn, turn again into a narrowing hall of bulrushes. Notice: floating diaper, watchful egret, six lily pads in a bunch. Smell: thick slime of sewage, torpid water nasty, implacable bacterial blooms. Our paddle-thrust increases, kicking up bugs and fish carcasses behind us. It's the two of us against her, and we've thrown our whole bodies into it: dunking and pulling, dunking and pulling with as much force as we can. But it's all no match for Madame Bovine. She slams her kayak into our canoe, sending our front end into an underwater boulder. She laughs fiendishly, grabbing at my arm. We manage to get away momentarily, our canoe a few metres ahead of her, when all of a sudden my friend calls a halt to the game. Our paddles cease, our canoe drifts. I know what he wants to do.

Enter: Amazonian cavern of dense forest overhang like the reaper's daggers. Enter: the loaded shotgun my friend brought for his final plunge. Enter: an unexpected exit wound on the other side of Madame Bovine's elephantine chest. A large pop and blood splatter. Then another pop in my friend's brains, self-inflicted. Scent of gunpowder and runoff. Two paddles without arms float carelessly. Silence, and I'm left alone in the oppressive heat. A kayak and canoe. A corroded soda can beside me. The bewitching twinkle of tiny flies on swamp, and three Canadian geese don't even flinch. It goes that fast.

# His July 13 at Mega Supermarket

He enters Mega Supermarket, wallet in his back pocket, grocery list stuffed beside it. Fruit section is first in the factory of foods, directs his shopping cart there. Up ahead, near the apples, pears and plums, *une petite femme* dressed to the nines in golden shimmer pantsuit and stilettos. "Well, hello young man…" Her voice is sultry and contrived, greets him with a wink as he approaches. Plastic bass woman with cat eyes reveals her age when she speaks; surgeons can do nothing for vocal chords. And her nails, long and red, bejewel old reptilian hands squeezing apples. Firm apples. Young apples. McIntosh shiny and waxy, and she glances at him with the flicker of thick mascara, "Beautiful, aren't they?" Overhead lighting is abrasive and raw; he can see every pull to her skin, the cake of whiteface and archaic blush, notices mildew on her upper lip. Fresh Produce Cougaress.

❧❧❧

Bakery alcove: hot and steamy, ovens maxed and lights blazing. Behind the counter, three sixteen-year-old girls half his age dressed in baker's hats and culinary lab coats. A convocation of bald eagles. Tight-lipped virginesses. Muffin-topped and young, they knead dough, ice cake, look up doe-eyed and ask what they can do for him. Like a wasp activating in the heat of summer, he's feverish and turned on, his pants liven with the yeasted bread, the sweltering bakery, the heat of sixteen candles.

"Oh…hmmm…" he hesitates, grabs a nearby package, "could you slice this for me?"

It's an oblong loaf that he whips around the edge of the counter. Thin, stumpy, and sallow – not quite a Parisian baguette, but it'll do.

"Um, we don't usually cut our mini-baguettes. It screws up the machine."

〜〜〜

In the dry goods aisle, granola bar boxes are colourful across the shelf like rainbow sprinkles on banana split spread-eagle. And an overwhelming array of Cherry Cream Oatmeal, Nanaimo Flax Bar, Yogurt Splattered Squash Puree. The one on his grocery list: Faux Blueberry Field – nutritious because it's fruity, a saviour because it's sugar-filled. Two packages secured in his metal cart, he looks down the aisle, the swarms of boxed delicacies immortally preserved. And there, on the periphery of cookies – that unmarked border before hot beverages – a shorthaired vixen, robust and glowing, stands analyzing the ingredients of Lipton Green Tea. On her: a miniskirt with beige owl print, plain white tank top, chunky blue necklace and large breasts like Melon Fruitcake Explosion. She turns and walks towards him, eyes still fixed on the tea box, softly brushes his shoulder with hers. Electricity. Fiery electric sex on two legs walking away.

❧❧❧

Meat department. All the sloppy chops and mountainous ground, the steaks and livers, the Styrofoam and shrinkwrap. He fingers a heap of minced pork, pushes his thumb inside making a moist dimple of meat, lifts the package to his nose and smells if it's fresh. *Delicious*. Expiration date: July 17. He doesn't know what constitutes freshness, but the pork feels soft and pliable, not too fatty, smells hygienically tangy. Afterwards he edges his way down to assorted chicken: three shelves of Caucasian flesh in different cuts – gizzard, drumstick, thigh, heart, wing. Reaches for a tray of two breasts strapped together in plastic, skin-on, bone-in. They look nubile and slippery, tissuey fat like melted candle wax, thick flaps of pallid skin. Tray goes straight into the cart.

⚅⚅⚅

Egg and dairy refrigerators contain mounds of reproductive by-products all housed in cartons and bags, and he loves the look of twelve eggs neatly in a row. Immaculately placed. Malformed prolate spheroids containing inner-gooiness, residual menstrual blood splatters on white, and every one of them screaming *FERTILITY! FERTILITY!* ready to be boiled or scrambled or opened with a spoon, scooped out with a hefty piece of buttered toast. He grabs two cartons, moves on to cheese. Grabs a brick of cheddar, moves on to butter. Grabs a slab of salted, moves on to milk. Whole. Creamy. He likes milk so fat he can stick his spoon in vertically. He loves that moment right before souring when milk is ripe and carnal, begs for either complete ingestion or rot, will rot if not ingested. He snatches a bag of three sacs, expiration date two days ago.

⚅⚅⚅

In the checkout line magazines frame hulking breasts in negligible clothing, show him the ins and outs of roly-poly, *HOW TO LOSE 30 POUNDS IN ONE WEEK*. He looks at the cashier five customers away, her dyed mahogany hair held back in a dinky bun too small to unravel and rub his head in. She looks fierce as a lightning strike, experienced, loose, razor sharp vagina dentata. For something gushier, he turns his eyes to the titanic ass directly in front of him in line – imagines celluloid bulges under inappropriate panties, sees the crack along jean hem and thinks of black holes, keloids, dynamite, parasitic growths, yeast infections, the confectionary aisle, the outhouse bucket, the diaphragm, gristle, plaque and a thousand bones shattering under killer orcinus. Finally it's his turn to place grocery items on the cashier conveyor belt: apples, mini-baguette, granola bars, pork, chicken, eggs, cheese, butter, milk. In front of him titanic ass inches up slightly, barely squeezing between chocolate bar rack and conveyor belt, lets out a giggle. It reminds him of Thanksgiving and he notices his minced pork sweating, pushes it away from the other items. A puddle of animal discharge left behind.

# Plungers, Porcelain, and Paltry Things

Sometimes the improbable is plunged from a toilet bowl. Stick the red rubber membrane in. Push. Peer inside the toilet like a crystal ball, and die of instant heart attack. Stroke. Unexpected trauma. So much inside that prophetic porcelain, such improbability – death becomes you.

Meet Maxine Francine-Ferez, nineteen-year-old Anglo-Montrealer, grew up in Hotel du Fort with her depressed father and heir to millions, Jacques.

Meet Jacques Francine-Ferez, Maxine's father. Well-groomed. A wearer of debonair suits. Black tailored beauties, always with a handkerchief in the front pocket, red as a toilet plunger. Jacques is a sour man. A fatalist. A self-deprecating father of one who drinks the Grey Goose stocked each day in his minibar. He loves Grey Goose. He also loves Maxine – their Prestige Suite covered in her drawings from kindergarten, every card she ever gave him for Father's Day, photos of her in front of their mini plastic Christmas tree, birthday parties, Easter egg hunts. His Maxine. His baby-girl Pumpkin who eats with her mouth open and laughs with her eyes closed.

Picture Klaus Francine-Ferez, Maxine's great-grandfather, owner and operator of a toilet plunger factory in Sherbrooke years ago, back when the province's piping system was "simply fatal" (Klaus' exact words), leading him to millions. He saw a need and filled it. Created cups of the best rubber, mechanized the craftsmanship with the latest technology. On his conveyer belts: stiff cups on sticks ready to cover toilet mouths across Quebec. His motto: *Plunge, Suction, Clear.*

Quality toilet plungers are a seemingly practical and generous contribution to humanity. And when other manufacturers were making multicoloured plungers in the '60s, pink plungers for the domestic housewife, and steel grey rubber with stained oak handles for the urban male, Klaus remained stead-fast with his reliable red. Red, he felt, was the best colour for a plunger. It stands out amid effluvial murk. It signals *EMERGENCY.* Most of all, a red plunger defuses embarrassment for those who have that naughty "monthly visitor" (Klaus' exact words).

Maxine's great-grandfather died at eighty-four due to what was deemed Rubber-Related Cancer. Maxine's grandfather died five years later at sixty-six due to what was deemed Rubber-Related Cancer. Maxine's father, who didn't work a day of his life in the plunger factory, sold the family business as soon as his own father died. Although he worries it's in his destiny, Maxine's father, at forty-nine, has no signs of Rubber-Related Cancer. He says, "I'll know for sure if I live past sixty-six."

Jacques and Maxine's home is exactly six hundred and twelve square feet, filled with hotel furniture, industrial-quality carpet, mini-fridge, electric stovetop but no oven, diminutive soaps and shampoos whenever Maxine requests them. Picture seventeen years in Hotel du Fort; Maxine is used to transient neighbours by now. She likes the rattle of the ice machine at night. She loves the concierges like extended family, thinks the security officers are her guardian angels. She was only two when the turrets and tailored lawns of Westmount were stripped from her. Life held such promise for Maxine in those early years. But then her mother left. And Jacques medicated himself with Novocain and Grey Goose. With nowhere else to go, Maxine lived for four months with her grandfather's sister while Daddy lay buried inside white-wall padding.

*C'est la vie*, as the old adage goes.

*C'est la vie* when Maxine would arrive home from school to find Jacques passed out in their whirlpool tub, faucet running, bubbles everywhere. *C'est la vie* when chambermaids were constant nannies, and Maxine would ask every beautiful guest swept into the hotel lobby if she was her mother. *C'est la vie* that Jacques and Maxine shared a queen-size bed until she was thirteen, at which point it became mandatory for all Prestige Suites to have a separate sofa bed. *C'est la vie* that Maxine's mother, a serpentine woman, was found dead and foaming at the mouth in Omaha three days before Maxine's fifteenth birthday. Apparently she drank five litres of bleach.

It's also simply *la vie* that Maxine's life would take a sudden and unexpected plunge, dredge up sudden and unexpected events. At nineteen we find her skimming through consignment shops along Boulevard Saint-Laurent. She wears a burgundy cloche hat, a white wool-felt poncho with large silver buttons, bleached pixie hair hidden, and wine-coloured lips. She fits right in with the rags and riches that surround her. Emaciated mannequins with hips jutted show off the latest treasures. Bejewelled purses hang from brass hooks, scarves in baskets. Marta's Kitsch-Caboodle Secondhand Store.

Picture Maxine, a tiny vitreous girl, glassy skin with golden undertone, and the rusty shopping cart in which hangers and clothes get tossed, wheels askew, powering forward, section to section to section. Picture translucent pixie in oversized vintage poncho making friends with a spandex lace top. In her cart: a ruched satin party dress from the '80s, laced bodice in watermelon pink, a pair of purl-stitched fuchsia legwarmers. The Ralph Lauren sweater in koala grey is ghastly, too much like a housecoat down to her knees, too manly. And someone else's hair is on the strapless sequin cocktail dress. Someone else's cat's hair in silver tufts across the ancient pea coat.

Picture her trying all of it on.

And fixed to the taupe blazer she threw in at the last minute, there's an angel pin – cheap imitation gold and diamonds, salvation pinned to the collar. And in the pockets of the shiny black bomber: Kleenexes and an unopened maxi-pad.

Maxine's daily history lesson: the past lives of secondhand clothes. An education of those *first*hands, those *other* hands. The hands that found each article of clothing immediately post-conception in department store nurseries. Those first-fingers that peeled each garment from the rack, spanked it on its ass and said: *This'll do*. Photographs have been taken in which these clothes were jubilantly worn by other bodies, captured there like ghosts. Moments of lust in which these clothes have been torn off, thrown on the floor, naked feet walking over them on the way to the bathroom later. And first kisses. Divorce. Hurricanes. Blizzards. Pregnancy. Church. Funerals. Maxine imagines it all, is sure the blood-red velvet blazer she bought three weeks ago was thrown off its owner mere seconds before she was defenestrated from an eighteenth-storey office. And the cloche hat Maxine wears today – at one time it belonged to a Cleopatra wannabe, a lady who painted her eyes like dazzling Egyptian goddesses, black charcoal makeup found on the hat's edges.

But among all the history – the infinite possibilities spawned from unadulterated ennui, the imaginative past lives of vintage garments that Maxine stews over and describes in graphic detail to her Grey-Goosed barely lucid father. Among all of this, Maxine could never imagine what's in the lining of Cream Chiffon Blouse, the blouse that makes its way into her awareness while she stands chewing bubblegum languidly in the checkout line, tapping her foot, customer after customer, four in front of her slow as the molasses her daddy left dripping in the whirlpool tub. Her bubblegum bubble pops and she turns her attention to an unexplored rack in the far corner. She sees the blouse hanging there, decides to try it on last minute, and thus changes the course of her life.

The blouse has grandmother-red lipstick stained on the collar, grandmother-scented *eau de toilette*. She tries it on in the narrow change room. Presses it against her skin, rubs the fabric, eyes herself in the mirror and hopes she's going to like it – *but alas*! The shoulders have too much *za-zam*, the buttons are boring. Waste of time, so picture Maxine throwing the blouse on the floor of the stall with listless force then resuming her place in the checkout line. Bubblegum blown into reckless bubbles again. Impatient foot tap resumes.

A few hours later: Maxine is twisting and wrenching in her hotel sofa  bed, contortive limbs, wild body-jerks. Cream Chiffon Blouse laced with abject virus. Cream Chiffon Blouse old and decrepit, storehouse for infectious calamity. Someone became a cadaver in Cream Chiffon Blouse. Someone wasted away wearing it.

Maxine feels nauseous and itchy. Her skin is inflamed, scores of calamitous bumps. Never before has such glassy translucence taken to the rouge of infection. Never has pixie-girl wanted to shave off her epidermis, knead out her nausea, extinguish feverous burning. And she's writhing in her hotel house. Fried and scratchy like maggots flailing around in old meat. Meanwhile Daddy Jacques eats *poisson frais du jour* at Le Paris restaurant downtown. He's within walking distance but Grey-Goosed to dizziness, and *poisson* is meant to be savoured.

When Jacques returns home three hours later, Maxine is barely verbal. Still writhing, she sees her father enter the suite and asks him to take her temperature. Her words slur like sewage drips from a garbage bag and Jacques is already on his knees shouting to the highest heavenly host, "Save my daughter! Save Maxine!"

Her back reminds him of bloodletting. Leeches. Suction cups ready to pop. She's red as blood pudding – or what Jacques imagines blood pudding to be like because he's never seen it before. And that texture! His baby girl's once delicate skin, silken as morning dew on an open field – ravaged now by the spiked wheels of some infection dump truck. An infection driving across the soft of her back and ruining all the lush grass, tearing up the soil. Leaving behind massively raised carbuncles and pustules and boils.

Most harrowing for Jacques: across Maxine's back he can't help but see those red rubber cups that have defined his entire existence. A series of toilet plungers without sticks. Red and rubbery. Raised and ready. Across her back: the same toilet plunging cup from which a few days later Maxine decides to elicit help. Handful of pills going into her mouth daily. Antibiotics up the wazoo to quell infection. Antipruritics for itch. Painkillers for frying ache. The doctor who did her biopsy said of her condition: "My dear, it only looks disastrous – just absolutely manic – but not to worry, it's not life-threatening. There will be four weeks of antibiotics – many antibiotics. Oh, and here's something for the itch."

A few days after, doped up on a drug cocktail, Maxine feels deathly.

In a stupor of painkillers, antipruritics, antibiotics, we find her fumbling around the bathroom for more pills. She feels bloated. Carnivorous indigestion nibbling on her insides. Organs impacted like overstuffed sausage. Inside her: a deli of jammed intestines. She wants relief. Some kind of soothing gastrointestinal care, then sleep. Picture Maxine's hands shaky and uncontrollable. Picture her fishing through the tub of sedatives and other medicinal wonders sitting on the shelf over the toilet bowl. Imagine having your eyes so filmy and medicated that labels on pill bottles make their contents look like candy – Tylenol are jujubes, Advil cinnamon hearts, Jacques' Novocain a bottle of soda pop.

Maxine takes the bottle of antibiotics – her "panacea" (Jacques' exact words) – and with wobbly fingers, fingers rattling with infection and drugs, she unscrews the lid. Shaky. Unnerving. Tips the bottle over. Pours. She's pouring antibiotics like a mound of gobstoppers but misses her palm completely. Maxine watches with patchy vision as all her gel-cap antibiotics fall into the toilet bowl. They float briefly, then sink inside the toilet mouth, sink lower out of sight.

Never do anything important over a toilet.

And it's 2:46am at the time. Jacques is knocked out: Grey Goose and Novocain – there's no rousing him. It's too early to call the doctor. Pharmacy is closed. Hotel maintenance is useless. Meanwhile Maxine is supposed to take two hundred milligrams of broad-spectrum antibiotic every hour on the hour. That's twelve hundred milligrams of missed pills until she can possibly get more.

So desperate and fucked up with a brain mangled by drugs. So itchy, feeling like she needs some kind of whole-body tail to swat away flies – *innumerable* flies – hundreds, thousands grazing on her skin, nibbling. She reaches for what she knows best, what's in her genetic makeup: The toilet plunger.

Maxine dunks her plunger into toilet water, fastens the pliable rubber cup to the toilet mouth, and pushes, full force, trying to suck up the antibiotics. *Where are those pills!* And she hums *row row row your boat, gently down the* – pushes harder – *stream, merrily merrily merrily merrily* – harder! – *life is but a dream!*

What Maxine doesn't know is that enthusiastic plunging can lead to wooden handles breaking. They don't make wooden handles like Klaus used to. And Maxine is pushing with her full pixie body, all her weight on one shoddy stick of pseudo-wood. And she's plunging, and she's pushing, and nothing is sucking up, no vomitus, no pills – when suddenly, without warning, wood stick snaps, and down goes Maxine's body. And there smacks Maxine's chin. And thus cracks Maxine's jaw. And her front teeth crumble snap with impact. And she bangs her head against the toilet paper holder, feels wood shards straight into her skin.

Has anyone ever plunged themselves to death? What an image for Jacques to find the next morning! Maxine's frail pixie body knocked unconscious, pustules, carbuncles and boils. And blood. Blood surfacing. Blood gushing. And a red rubber cup floats loose in the toilet water. Scattered antibiotics, half-dissolved, swirl there too.

Except Maxine doesn't die.

She's not dead.

Picture Maxine, splayed across the bathroom, a bumpy red carpet. She's *unconscious*, sure. Cheek dab-smack on a bathroom tile. Teeth abandoned on the floor. But not dead. Picture Maxine not dead. See Jacques stumble into the bathroom hours later, still asleep, eyes half-closed, unaware his beloved daughter is lying in front of him. Consider that Jacques doesn't know *WHAT THE FUCK* when he steps forward and accidentally falls over her strewn body. He doesn't get hurt. He's thinking: Towels, probably a pile of wet towels. Rubs his eyes to see what's going on.

"*Maxine?*"

Jacques is up, pokes his daughter, pulls her body into a lethargic seated position and slaps her face to see if she'll wake up.

"PUMPKIN?"

He's screaming to Madonna and God and Shiva and the fucking Grey Goose he guzzled last night. He drags Maxine into the main room, calls the front desk. It's 12:00pm, checkout time, chaos: no one answers. He hits Maxine's face again, sticks his finger into one of her neck boils, checks for a pulse.

Is there a pulse?

Jacques feels nothing. And on her wrist, another boil. On her chest, a large carbuncle. Maxine's heartbeat can't come through all that nasty wreckage.

In desperation, Jacques calls 911. Words barely lucid in the phone. Everything slurred and sewage and like bilious waste in a toilet bowl. The dispatcher can't understand anything he says; she thinks it's a prank and hangs up.

In desperation, Jacques is pacing the room. Sofa bed, kitchenette, Maxine's pictures and cards and photographs.

In desperation, Jacques opens the sliding door, onto the balcony, throws what's left of the red rubber plunger onto Rue du Fort. Gathers up all the wood shards, throws them out too.

In desperation, Jacques runs back to the bathroom, gobbles up Maxine's antipruritics, painkillers and his Novocain. Chases it all with Grey Goose.

Picture Jacques in desperation lying supine beside Maxine on industrial-quality hotel carpet. His body vibrating, mind swirling, mouth foaming like his ex-wife's did out in Omaha.

Picture one last spasm. And Jacques Francine-Ferez is dead. A rubber-related accident.

Maxine comes to three hours later. It's afternoon. Housekeeping time. A chambermaid knocks on the door, knocks Maxine out of her plunger-induced coma. She wakes up, body in shock, adrenaline pumping and numbing. She doesn't feel her missing teeth, or her skin gashes, boils and carbuncles, or the head trauma that kept her comatose for over twelve hours. Instead she sees Jacques spread across hotel carpet, white froth like icing flattened on his face, dry and pooled on the ground. Maxine lets out a hideous, boil-bursting scream. A scream that has the chambermaid break hotel rules, scramble for the room key, and run into the suite uninvited. She screams too.

Picture the chambermaid – stout woman, hair gelled slick-back in a tight bun on top of her head – screaming and wailing, rushing over to Maxine, helping Maxine up, crying for help, for someone to come, some kind of salvation. Half-conscious, Maxine contemplates a dull knife across her wrists, veins releasing and her body strewn over Jacques in a staggering *Romeo and Juliet* finale. But soon the hotel suite swells with police officers, medical professionals, forensic investigators. There's no dull knife through pixie wrists. No begging for mercy over Jacques' frosted corpse. If Maxine wanted to kill herself, there wasn't enough time, the sequence of events was too quick: Chambermaid rescue. 911. Emergency personnel. Trauma unit. Then Maxine lying vegetative in the Montreal General Hospital, body wrapped in gauzy dressings. Morphine drip. A cross over her bed. No visitors.

Hotel staff clean up the mess later that week. Tidy the suite for new guests. Take down Maxine's drawings, photographs and Father's Day cards. Send Jacques' clothes to secondhand stores along Boulevard Saint-Laurent – all his debonair suits and ties and handkerchiefs. And his vats of Novocain are flushed down the toilet bowl. Grey Goose restocked in the minibar.

Picture the weeks it takes for police investigators to piece together what happened. Imagine Maxine, four months later, head in a daze. It's been a daze. The last four months, a daze of sifting through racks at nondescript vintage stores. Living in a damp basement apartment in Mile End. Black nails and ruby lips and oversized retro coats. In her mouth: a row of false teeth. Her Cream Chiffon infection: vanished. No vestigial bump or blemish. Only a pulse beating through clear-liquid skin again. And it beats faster today, these four months later. Picture it beating faster, then all of a sudden nearly stopping. Walking by a men's secondhand store, beautifully crisp afternoon, Maxine just happens to turn her head briefly and glances in the storefront window. There, suited on a hip-jutting male mannequin, she's sure she sees a suave black blazer with something poking up from the front pocket. Red as a toilet plunger.

# HERKIMER

*Friday March 5<sup>th</sup> 1976, 9:00am: Stratus clouds. Zorki #2 camera functioning A+.*

꧁꧁꧁

Jane: "He left the coffee machine on again! He'll burn down the fucking house!"

Jane always yells at Kate. When Kate hears Jane yell, her body calms. It's a sign of Jane's affection.

Down the road from Jane and Kate, Frank pets a stray cat with the same hand his wedding ring is on.

Frank: "I WILL CALL HER LIBBY."

Libby the cat is a him, not a her. He is black and has a floppy, loose-hanging belly that looks like it has carried seventeen litters of kittens. In all his excitement, Frank is reminded of Mr. Potato Head and is sure that Libby is half kangaroo. He can't wait to show Kate and Jane.

Jane: "*Jee*-zus, Frank! Why the hell did you bring that thing in here?"

CCC

Today Zorki's Zorki #2 is functioning at an A+ level, which means all parts are working properly. Zorki has three Zorkis and all three of them are always functioning at an A+. He chose to use Zorki #2 today because yesterday he used Zorki #1 and tomorrow he intends on using Zorki #3. No matter which Zorki he uses, when Zorki takes his daily photograph he unintentionally captures the rightmost corner of Myrtle and Ralph's roof in the leftmost corner of his photo. He doesn't like or dislike this fact and makes no effort to change the location of his daily shot.

Myrtle and Ralph's house is across the street from Zorki and one house to left. It has three bedrooms and is considered an "empty nest" by friends and family. Two years ago, Myrtle and Ralph wasted no time in converting their children's bedrooms into: 1) A personal workout space for Myrtle, 2) What Myrtle refers to as the Special Room. The latter is used only on what Myrtle refers to as "special" occasions. While Myrtle and Ralph have at least one photograph of their two children on every wall of their home, there are no photographs of them in the Special Room. Instead Myrtle and Ralph have hung large mirror panels on two of the four walls.

ᒻᒻᒻ

On the opposite side of town, Gigi's face is covered in that type of pallid, cratered skin one imagines the face of a girl named Gigi would have. Her hair is chin length, overprocessed and wispy, and she uses hydrogen peroxide to bleach her eyebrows. She has unusual plans for today and feels queasy about it.

ᒻᒻᒻ

Jane: "KATE! – Your brother brought a fucking cat in here!"

*She loves me.*

Jane: "KAAATE?"

Libby the cat is skittish but likes Frank. Frank likes touching Libby. When Frank touches Libby, he is very careful not to get his wedding ring stuck in Libby's fur. The black colour of Libby's fur reminds Frank of Myrtle's hair after Ralph would scold him. Whenever Frank got in trouble, Myrtle would hug him and he'd stick his face in her hair. It always smelled of hyacinth.

Kate: "Awwww, come on... she's cute, babe, and Frankie really seems to like her."

Jane: "I don't care! I don't want a fucking animal in here!"

Frank continues to rub Libby and is oblivious to the argument going on between Jane and Kate. He is very good at tuning things out and focusing on one object. Today his focus is on Libby. Frank sticks his nose in Libby's fur to see if it smells like hyacinth. It doesn't. Frank thinks it smells like sardines, and conjectures that Libby must have lived by Lake Ontario at one time. Frank thinks Lake Ontario is stinky like sardines because Ralph told him it was. He kisses Libby.

Kate: "Awww – see? Look how darling that was, Jane… Frankie has a friend."

Kate, Jane and Frank live on the north corner of Herkimer Street. Myrtle and Ralph live three houses from the south corner of Herkimer Street. Myrtle and Ralph's house is two kilometres away from Kate, Jane and Frank's house, and even though it is impossible, Kate often worries that Myrtle and Ralph will overhear her fighting with Jane. Kate surmises that if Myrtle and Ralph heard the two of them fighting, she'd be "found out." Down the street, however, Myrtle and Ralph couldn't care less about what Kate is doing. Today is a special occasion for them. They have already prepared the Special Room by cleaning the mirrors with Windex and arranging the pillows. Now they're in the midst of preparing the dining room table. Myrtle instructs

Ralph to place the cutlery while she folds the nap-kins.

*&&&*

Across town, Gigi has been in front of the bathroom mirror all morning. Her face is covered in thick white makeup that fills in all her gaps. Gigi imagines her face like the bumpy shale she would drive by up north when she was a child. Her parents would bring her to Midland every year and they'd camp by the water. Those trips feel like an eternity ago for Gigi. She wonders where the years go and whether she should go out today. Maybe she should cancel her plans? She could say she doesn't feel well, which isn't technically a lie.

*&&&*

Zorki is short for Zorkimidian. Zorkimidian wasn't a real name until his mother, Dolores Lexter, dreamt of it while hallucinating. Dolores had taken three tabs of LSD when she says a male angel appeared and sang the word Zorkimidian to her. There is only one person in the world named Zorkimidian. His name is Zorki Lexter and he lives on Herkimer Street.

❧❧❧

Myrtle: "The knives go on the *right* side, sweetheart."

❧❧❧

As brother and sister, Kate and Frank share approximately fifty percent of the same genes. They both have red hair, green eyes and freckles. Each one found learning to read difficult (Frank still does) and both like to be outdoors. Frank is triple the size of Kate, but Kate blames this on his medication and assumes he'd be the same size as her if he didn't have to take it. Also, they both share the same favourite meal: broccoli casserole. Kate's feelings of responsibility for Frank, however, are not genetically predisposed. These feelings are a result of watching Ralph kick Frank in the ear repeatedly when Kate and Frank were young.

Frank: "LIBBY LOVES ME."

Kate loves her father but hates it when he calls Frank a moron. Kate's father hasn't called Frank a moron for two years. Kate has noticed a change in her father's mood lately. He seems happier. She asked him about it once and he said it must be the exercise he's getting.

༄༄༄

Across town, Gigi mists herself in the Chanel No. 5 Ralph gave her. She puts on the cocktail dress that Myrtle says makes her look *sexy*. Should she go? She reapplies her pale pink lipstick and thinks maybe she should cancel.

༄༄༄

Myrtle: "*Toute suite*, sweetheart. She'll be here soon."

༄༄༄

The name "Zorkimidian" was conceived while Dolores was on LSD. Nine months later, Zorki Lexter was conceived while Dolores was drunk. That was over fourteen years ago and for fourteen years Zorki Lexter has hated his name.

When he was four, Zorki asked Dolores where his father was. Zorki was a very observant child and wondered why he didn't have a man pulling him by the ear down Herkimer Street the same way Frank did. Dolores, wanting to be as discreet as possible, told Zorki that his father died in "The War" and was in heaven. "Where's heaven?" Zorki asked her. "Up there." Dolores pointed to the clouds in the sky. Soon

Zorki noticed that "heaven" changed every day. Some days it was blue, others black, and sometimes it contained no clouds at all. He was going to ask Dolores where heaven went on those days when all the clouds were missing, but decided it might make her sad.

&&&

Across town, Gigi brings a tiny silver spoon full of powder up to her nose. She snorts then pouts in the mirror. Should she go?

&&&

Jane: "Kate! It's a mangy animal, probably full of parasites! Tell him to get it the fuck out of here. You promised!"

*God I love her.*

&&&

Today Frank has decided Libby will marry Mr. Potato Head instead of Barbie. Frank likes weddings ever since he got married two years ago. When he got married, Frank wore a powder blue suit with a white ruffled tuxedo shirt. After the wedding, Frank became obsessed with this outfit and didn't take it off for two months. Kate worries that he might do the same thing with Libby, but she also thinks having a friend to take care of could be good for Frank.

Kate: "Janey, I think it could be good for him. I *really* do."

Jane: "Oh you and your fucking love affair with your brother!"

Kate: "Shh! Jane, *please* stop yelling… You know how I feel about us yelling in here… the walls are thin…"

Jane: "Get over it, Kate. You're parents aren't going to walk by and even if they do who gives a shit? I'll go right down there and tell them – I don't care if they know."

Down the street Ralph pinches Myrtle's ass. Myrtle is bent over with her head in the oven checking on the broccoli casserole. Almost all photographs of their two children have been taken down today and stored in the pantry. The only one that remains is a photograph of Frank and Jane at the wedding.

❦❦❦

Across town, Gigi brings the tiny silver spoon up to her nose and snorts again. She's going to go.

❦❦❦

One Christmas when Zorki was ten Dolores decided to buy him everything that had his name on it. This consisted of three cameras and a plain navy T-shirt Dolores had custom-made with "Zorki" written across the front diagonally. On the label of this T-shirt, Dolores put the words: "Zorkimidian Clothing Unlimited." Zorki refused to wear his T-shirt, but decided to document each day of his life using his new Zorki cameras starting the next day, Boxing Day.

It took Zorki three hours to decide how he would document his own life. After seeing Frank emerge naked from Myrtle and Ralph's house that Christmas 1972 and precede to lather snow all over himself, the lampposts and cars, and after witnessing Ralph scream then kick naked Frank in the ear minutes later, Zorki decided to take photographs of the clouds. The clouds were where his father lived and Zorki reasoned that taking a photo of them each day would be how he'd get to know him. Later that Christmas evening Ralph locked Frank in the cellar and asked God why he gave him a moron for a son.

❦❦❦

Gigi locks her apartment door and walks to the bus stop. Her coat is oversized and made of fake leopard fur. A friend gave it to her. She likes the way the fur puffs up to her face. She also likes how big it is wrapped around her tiny frame. It makes her feel safe. When she reaches the bus stop, Gigi lights up a cigarette and waits.

❦❦❦

Jane: "You promised, Kate! – If I went through with everything and we all lived together, you promised shit like this wouldn't happen. You promised you'd stand up for me!"

*Can we just make love?*

❦❦❦

The bus comes.

❦❦❦

Zorki takes one photograph of the clouds each morning at 9:00am. He keeps all his photographs in a journal. On the front cover of this journal, Zorki has written *THE ZORKI NEWS BIBLE* in black ink. Outside of his one daily photograph, Zorki has never taken a picture with any of his Zorki cameras, or any camera for that matter. He's never thought to.

❧❧❧

Myrtle: "I think I see her coming down the alley, sweetheart!"

❧❧❧

Walking down the alley, Gigi likes feeling safe inside her big fur coat. The snow crunches under her feet. As she walks, she thinks only of the snow crunching and how safe she feels in her fur coat.

❧❧❧

Myrtle: "Yes, yes, it's *her*! How do I look, sweetheart?"

❧❧❧

Gigi arrives.

❧❧❧

Frank considers what Libby will wear when she gets married to Mr. Potato Head. In his mind he imagines the pink dress his mother wore to his own wedding. He thinks he should ask his mother if he could borrow her pink dress and sew it to Libby's size. The thought of this makes Frank very happy. Frank decides to give Libby a hug and squeezes him gently. Libby likes when Frank squeezes him. Frank likes squeezing Libby. On the living room couch Kate squeezes Jane's thigh.

❧❧❧

Myrtle: "Well, don't you look *beautiful*! *Wel*come! Here, let me take that *big* coat of yours."

❧❧❧

Frank was born in 1952, a decade before Zorki. Despite living on the same street as Zorki all his life, Frank has no idea who Zorki is. One day three years ago, Dolores Lexter asked Ralph if Frank and Zorki could be friends. They were the only two boys living on Herkimer Street in 1973. In 1973, Zorki was eleven and Frank was twenty-one. Despite the age difference, Ralph said OK. He was glad to get rid of his son for the day.

Accordingly, Frank and Zorki had a playdate during which Zorki introduced Frank to Mr. Potato Head. Hitherto Frank had only played with his sister's old Barbie dolls, and was very excited by the fact that he could change Mr. Potato Head's face. Frank became obsessed with Mr. Potato Head that day and when he left Zorki's house at dinnertime, he stuck Mr. Potato Head under his sweater and brought him home. Frank doesn't remember any of this. He doesn't know who Zorki is or that he stole Zorki's only Mr. Potato Head. Instead, Frank thinks he found Mr. Potato Head on a neighbour's front lawn much the same way he found Libby today.

In Zorki's journal, it reads: *February 27th 1973, 9:00am: Cumulus clouds. Zorki #1 camera functioning A+.*

Underneath, Zorki taped his daily photograph. In the leftmost corner of this photograph you can see the tip of Frank's frizzy red afro. Frank was arriving at the time. Along the margin of the notebook, Zorki later wrote: *Today Frank Miller stole the Mr. Potato Head Mom gave me when I was six.*

๑๑๑

Myrtle: "Oh, sit down, sit down – make yourself at home. Sweetheart? Can you please bring the wine?"

๑๑๑

There are three pillows set neatly in a row on the bed in Myrtle and Ralph's Special Room. They smell like Myrtle's hyacinth *eau de toilette*.

❦❦❦

Myrtle: "So, how have you been? You look *beautiful* by the way. Just *beautiful!*"

❦❦❦

There are four condoms slipped between the mattress and box spring in Myrtle and Ralph's Special Room. Myrtle's negligee hangs over a bedrail.

❦❦❦

Myrtle: "Now, is that the sparkling wine, sweetheart? I had hoped for the *sparkling* this afternoon."

❦❦❦

With her middle and index fingers, Kate rubs Jane in small circles. Across the room Frank continues to squeeze Libby.

Frank: "LIBBY IS GETTING MARRIED SOON."

❦❦❦

Myrtle: "Well, then. Let's move into the dining room, shall we? Sweetheart, please dim the lights just a smidgen."

❦❦❦

Jane whimpers slightly. Frank squeezes Libby harder.

❦❦❦

Myrtle: "Oh, *thank you*, sweetheart. You two catch up while I fetch the casserole."

❦❦❦

Kate uses two hands now.

Jane: "Don't touch me like that when your brother brought a fucking animal in here and you won't do anything about it. You always choose him over me!"

*She's excited.*

❦❦❦

When Ralph touches her hand from across the dining room table, Gigi feels excited. She asks Ralph who the people are in the photograph on the wall and he tells her it's his son and daughter-in-law at their wedding two years ago. He doesn't want to tell her the truth; it would alarm Gigi, and Myrtle might overhear. Then Gigi asks how old his son is and blushes when she learns they are the same age. Twenty-four. In the kitchen Myrtle pokes the casserole. It's ready.

*CCC*

Jane: "I'm *leaving*, Kate. When I get back, that thing better be gone!"

Jane puts on her winter boots and coat. She can still feel Kate's fingers rubbing her and wants to take Kate upstairs to make love. Jane knows, however, that if she does Frank will continue getting away with everything. Jane thinks Frank gets away with everything because of his condition. Doctors call Frank's condition Educable Mental Retardation. Ralph has always blamed Myrtle for Frank's Educable Mental Retardation. Ralph says Myrtle's family is crazy. For twenty-two years Ralph has resented Myrtle. Two years ago everything changed.

*CCC*

Myrtle: "Presenting…my famous broccoli casserole. I hope you like cheese!"

&&&

Zorki eats a ham and cheese sandwich and stares out the front window of his house. He didn't want to go to school today so he didn't have to. Dolores Lexter always gives in to Zorki. Consequently, Zorki has spent his day eating and reading about space. He is currently taking a break.

Zorki sees a lady walk by. He recognizes her as Jane, the woman who is married to Frank. He wonders what she sees in Frank and why Frank's sister lives with them.

&&&

Myrtle: "Oh, eat up, eat as much as you want. Here, do you want a second helping?"

&&&

According to the commentary in THE ZORKI NEWS BIBLE, the first girl was two years ago. Zorki would see her leaving when he took his daily photograph. One morning Zorki overheard Myrtle and

Ralph say goodbye to her, calling her by name: *Lana*.
Zorki wasn't sure how to spell Lana so he wrote it
phonetically. Recently Zorki has noticed Gigi. Zorki
supposes that Gigi is the second.

❧❧❧

Myrtle: "There's *lots* of casserole!"

❧❧❧

Frank starts to cry because Jane left. He forgets he
is holding Libby.

❧❧❧

Myrtle: "More sparkling wine?"

❧❧❧

Frank squeezes Libby harder. He forgets Libby is a
cat.

❧❧❧

Myrtle: "More?"

☾☾☾

Frank squeezes Libby harder.

☾☾☾

Myrtle: "Shall we move upstairs then?"

☾☾☾

Frank cries and squeezes until Libby can't wail anymore.

☾☾☾

Myrtle: "I think we *shall*."

☾☾☾

There is a loud popping noise.

☾☾☾

Kate: "FRAAAAANK!"

☾☾☾

The three of them go upstairs.

⟪⟪⟪

Kate: "Frank, how *could* you?"

⟪⟪⟪

Zorki waves to Jane but Jane doesn't notice. She's thinking about making love to Kate. As Jane passes Kate's parents' house, she wonders whether she should tell them the truth. Jane posits that if Kate's parents learned the truth, Frank would move back home and leave her alone.

⟪⟪⟪

They undress.

⟪⟪⟪

Myrtle: "Oh, look how beautiful she is, sweetheart! Just *look!*"
    Myrtle kisses her neck.

⟪⟪⟪

Zorki watches Jane walk down the street to the corner then abruptly turn around.

❦❦❦

Frank: "LIBBY NO. NO LIBBY, NO! NO!"

❦❦❦

In the Special Room, Gigi sees Myrtle kissing her pale naked body in the mirror panels on the wall. She thinks she looks skinny and gross compared to Myrtle and Ralph. All she can smell is hyacinth and the broccoli casserole on Myrtle's breath.

❦❦❦

Kate: "I can't believe you just did that. Frankie, you – that's disgusting… I can't believe—"

❦❦❦

The three of them hear a knock on the door. Myrtle ignores it and continues kissing Gigi. Ralph is cross-legged on the floor touching himself.

❦❦❦

At this point both Kate and Frank are crying. Kate wants to get towels to help her brother clean up Libby, but she feels sick.

❧❧❧

Now the doorbell.

❧❧❧

Myrtle: "Oh! I wonder who that can be? Sweetheart?"

❧❧❧

The doorbell rings again.

Myrtle: "Oh, rather *determined* aren't we? I'll go see who it is then. Sweetheart? I'll be back in a jiffy."

❧❧❧

Myrtle wraps a blanket around her naked body haphazardly and tiptoes downstairs. Once in the family room, she peers out the window and sees Jane at the front door. Myrtle wonders why her daughter's girlfriend is at her house, and although it is rude to do so, she decides not to answer the door. Outside, Jane is too focused on the door being answered to notice Myrtle in the large window to her right.

❧❧❧

Kate: "Frankie, I just – I just can't be here right now. You're going to have to deal with this yourself, I—"

❧❧❧

Zorki is across the street wondering why Myrtle is looking at Jane through a window wearing only a blanket. He also wonders why she won't open the door for Jane and why Jane seems so angry.

❧❧❧

Kate leaves the house sobbing. She goes after Jane.

❧❧❧

Myrtle has always hated Jane, ever since she saw Jane and her daughter making out in the garage. Myrtle never told Kate that she saw her. She also never told Ralph because she was afraid he'd blame her for it. Ralph always blames her for everything.

When Myrtle suggested they make the Special Room two years ago, after Jane and Frank got married and both children moved out, Ralph became a lot more manageable for Myrtle.

⸭⸭⸭

Frank: "NO! KATE NO GO, KATE."

⸭⸭⸭

Being somewhat curious, Zorki decides to use Zorki #3 to take photographs of what he's seeing. Zorki has never used his cameras to take photographs of anything other than his daily photograph. He feels excited by the idea.

⸭⸭⸭

*Friday March 5$^{th}$ 1976, 6:06pm: Zorki #3 functioning at A+. Jane Miller stands on the front porch of Myrtle and Ralph Miller's house while Kate Miller runs up the front porch towards her. Myrtle Miller is in the front window wearing a blanket.*

⸭⸭⸭

*Friday March 5$^{th}$ 1976, 6:06pm: Kate Miller hugs Jane Miller. Myrtle Miller is still in the front window wearing a blanket.*

❧❧❧

*Friday March 5$^{th}$ 1976, 6:07pm: Jane Miller is telling Kate Miller something and Kate Miller is nodding her head. Frank Miller runs down the street towards them with dark red all over his arms and chest (blood?). Myrtle Miller is leaving the front window.*

❧❧❧

*Friday March 5$^{th}$ 1976, 6:07pm: Kate Miller opens the front door of Myrtle and Ralph Miller's house. Jane Miller has her hand on Kate Miller's shoulder. Frank Miller continues running down the street with red all over himself. His arms are flying around in the air. He looks upset. It is still unclear what the red is. Myrtle Miller is gone from the front window.*

❧❧❧

*Friday March 5$^{th}$ 1976, 6:07pm: Kate Miller and Jane Miller step inside. Frank Miller is nearly at*

*Myrtle and Ralph Miller's house. He is yelling some-thing. I cannot hear what he's saying.*

છછછ

*Friday March 5$^{th}$ 1976, 6:08pm: Kate Miller turns around and sees Frank Miller at the bottom of the porch. Jane Miller doesn't move.*

છછછ

*Friday March 5$^{th}$ 1976, 6:08pm: Frank Miller walks up the porch. Kate Miller is still turned facing him. Jane Miller has her back to them and is saying some-thing to someone inside the house (Myrtle?). I cannot hear what she's saying.*

છછછ

*Friday March 5$^{th}$ 1976, 6:08pm: Kate Miller moves farther into the house so Frank Miller can enter. Jane Miller is gone from the shot.*

છછછ

*Friday March 5$^{th}$ 1976, 6:08pm: Everyone is in the house.*

❧❧❧

Friday March 5$^{th}$ 1976, 6:08pm: Kate Miller closes the door behind them.

❧❧❧

Friday March 5$^{th}$ 1976, 7:56pm: A frilly pink dress is thrown onto Myrtle and Ralph Miller's front lawn from a second-storey window. It looks like it has been ripped. Everyone is still in the house.

❧❧❧

Friday March 5$^{th}$ 1976, 8:07pm: The pink dress is still on Myrtle and Ralph Miller's front lawn. Everyone is still in the house.

❧❧❧

Friday March 5$^{th}$ 1976, 8:57pm: The pink dress is still on Myrtle and Ralph Miller's front lawn. Everyone is still in the house. A lady and a little girl (I think they live somewhere on Herkimer?) are nailing a poster on the lamppost in front of my house.

❧❧❧

*Friday March 5$^{th}$ 1976, 8:59pm: The pink dress is still on Myrtle and Ralph Miller's front lawn. Everyone is still in the house. The lady and little girl have left. The poster has a picture of a black cat on it. I cannot read what it says.*

❧❧❧

*Friday March 5$^{th}$ 1976, 9:00pm: The pink dress is still on Myrtle and Ralph Miller's front lawn. Everyone is still in the house. The poster rips slightly in the wind.*

# Uterine Kisses

In my mother the uterine walls glistened, a thick plastic shielding keeping cicadas away. I could hear only hums through synthetic womb ducts, only cicada love songs in artificial composition. Because my first midsummer cicadas were electric: the mumblings of wombs plugged in, wombs turned on, wombs dilated and full, cradling sacs of the proto-human, the *pre*human, malformed lumps like potatoes with eyeballs and quivering roots. One potato per womb and the cradle was warm, the cradle fed, nourished, oxygenated. And through tubes and plastic and electricity, I was alive.

July 16, I was alive.

With uterine kisses from an incubator. With gestation and only one heartbeat. I was alive and the world wasn't ready for me. I was alive and my eyes opened too soon. And it's a sunny July afternoon twenty-four years later. Here I am, behind vitreous flesh again, back inside a man-made belly that oxygenates, kept alive with tubes and wires. Somewhere in the hospital a girl sings, just softly and infrequently enough that no one will tell her to stop. She is my window towards Camelot. My will to live.

❦❦❦

IV drip: the necessary auxiliary, and we unite on hospital cotton. Our intravenous marriage, our love consummated in a hospital bedroom, my veins glowing till death do us part. Days are spent attached to one another, my body curled on bedsheets, flesh perspiring.

Bedpan: luxury bathroom – I don't have to get up to shit. Cold metal against my skin is a pick-me-up when I'm stoned on morphine, can't move.

Hospital linens: sweaty and vile. My sweat rancid, the waste of cellular lust, my cells' lust propagating vast armies. And what violent propagations! What anomalous propagations! – with ten-foot giants and cannibal cells and cells with razor claws. Cells upon cells upon cells marching the womb of my brain, armies of them in the cradle where skull makes cap, pushing brains to the outskirts, lobes mashed into skull bone, and my head aches, and my brain hurts. Ophthalmic migraine. Glioblastoma multiforme. Womb-vision resurrected.

This time my womb has flowers. Snapdragons. Lilies. Two sunflowers from my dad sit on my bedside table. I'm floating around in a kaleidoscope, a cylinder of mirrors containing scattered petals, debauched mouths, my vision distorted. Then sometimes the magnification of warning stickers. Other times the distortion of electrical plugs plugged in. I can't trust what I see and my brain is dying. In my new womb I'm embryonic towards death.

⟅⟅⟅

Twenty-four years ago I came into the world demanding more. Sperm met egg and I was ready to exist. I exploded atoms and cells back then, blossomed molecular infinities, my passion inviolable. It's like I knew. Even then, as a prehuman, even at that bloodless moment of flesh to vitreous womb, mother to incubator, even *then* I knew. And that more I wanted, that more I was determined to have, was Love. Always Love. But not a balding Love of terms and conditions. Instead: Love because it could be no other way. Love because it's in our bones.

With Jack I thought it was love.

I studied it, tried to know all of it. Three-am conversations of the soul with him under our sea mist glittering above. Our sea mist: a white mesh canopy we won at a bazaar. Our bed: a single mattress with one pillow, bodies curled into one, one half-brain speaking to the other. And curled like that, sometimes we'd attach together, him inside me from behind while synapses fired, sparks from one lobe to the next.

But love with Jack wasn't real.

None of it was. Instead, a realness like potatoes growing under glass. Real as feeding at the end of a tube. And those years of twenty-one and twenty-two, just imprints on my cells now. Just images dying with my brain. They swirl around like the melodies of Virginia Woolf midsummer. Tennyson Sundays. Months of Dostoevsky. And I love Edna St. Vincent Millay when it's raining, my heart nostalgic for things she writes but I've never known. My whole life like that: always an aching nostalgia for what I'll never know.

Never *get* to know.

Central Park's Shakespeare's Garden early autumn. London in the sunshine. Making a baby. Grandchildren. All the books unread. All the words unwritten. Sweat of another sweaty mid-June leg pressed against mine in the Paris underground. Metro car rattling. Calves smack. Parisian crepes filled with chocolate and berries. Italian gelato in a tiny back alley.

I'll never know this.

And every molecule of a moment, all those fine particles happening in every second of life, they'll keep turning and renewing and growing without me. And it's like I've always known this. Like my own cells try to compensate for years lost. I came into the world demanding more. More time. Please. Just one more year. One more chance at love. I want to carry my life in a knapsack. Feel Vietnam in the winter. Hang Christmas lights in a Manhattan apartment. And what is it like to see the world from above? Does it make you feel small? I want to feel small, but part of that smallness. I want to feel significant.

Please, just give me one more chance. Another year. Some love. Please. Some time and someone to love me as I waste away on this hospital bed; to hold my hand and kiss me while my brain swells and my cells fuck, and my cells bear more cells, and my skull becomes heavy! and my skull hurts! – It's like Paris or Die. New York City or Die. Like: Throw-Off-My-Hospital-Robes-and-March-Outside-into-the-Sunshine or Die. Restlessness, because every day is the same thing. Why am I even alive, then? July 16 – why? Why a birthday when I was never actually supposed to live? Fifty years ago I would've died before I was even born. No incubator placentas. No potatoes in plastic sacs. No artificial cicada love songs. Only hums of pretty little nurses. Hums trying to put real humans to sleep.

And I know Dad loves me. I know he does, that's why he can't come visit me. And he gave me two sunflowers! Dad loves me and he gave me two sunflowers, plucked right from the backyard garden. Dad? I'll never swing on the wooden swing you built me and hung from the willow tree in our backyard. And I'll never see the sunflowers wave or hear the cicadas loving between stems and grass, and I'll never feel my feet pointing straight to heaven in the midsummer sunshine, or hit soft ground while I run to you.

I'll never run.

And now I'm back in the womb again. My artificial womb where hums aren't real, aren't bugs in love. Where my garden has no roots but instead floats in water, flowers surviving in jars, glass wombs of their own. And now the wild colours are coming back. Insane twists of light and image and I'm terrified – I squeeze my mattress. I squirm. My IV pulls, and it hurts, and I wish someone were here to hold me, to be with me while I'm twenty-four. While I die.

Does anyone know what that's like? To feel like you don't have much time? – I ask this to the nurse yesterday between spoonfuls of chocolate hospital-pudding. She's twenty-two, fresh out of college. I ask her: Do you ever feel like your life will be short? – And she giggles nervously, pudding spills from the spoon. Nurses never like to talk about inevitability. It's in their handbook: Do not talk with patient about patient's imminent death. Do not talk to patient about death. Feed patient pudding and giggle, because death doesn't exist.

And she'll end her shift at 10:00pm. She'll go home to her big comfortable bed, snuggle with her boyfriend, forget all about my kind of inevitability. Because I'm just a footnote in her handbook. The tragic case of an early-twenties girl with a brain capsizing. Too many cells. Too little room. And there's nothing she can do to make it better. So instead she greets me each day with those concerned stares, those infantilizing grins telling me to smile and be happy and Have a Great Day! Or: How are you feeling today? How are you doing? How *are* you? – How am *I*? I'm fucking beautiful, thank you. My ass isn't as itchy today because the night nurse powdered it for me. My IVs are snug and only pinching slightly. And the morphine makes me feel *real* fine. Oh, by the way, all the distortions around me, I've embraced them. Your fragmented smile, I've embraced it. And I love your fragmented smile. I love your jagged teeth and my kaleidoscope vision, and I love being here with these nice cotton sheets, these foul smells, and the ease with which I can shit and pee. I love shitting and peeing in the bed where I live.

Guess what?

Some guy just puked right in front of my door and I didn't even wince. Because there's no wincing left when you're twenty-four and live each day in a hospital. When smells of artificial lemon and regurgitated meatloaf tickle nostrils, and you don't notice. When someone's last wails shriek through the night-time, and you barely hear. And all I have left are my black flashes, my lightning blinks, because the centre of my vision cuts in and out all day long. My lighthouse in the fog. My warning sign: *DANGER* up ahead, when the blinks get too much to bear. *DANGER*, when an entire person is missing from my vision. And I'm scared. My skull throbs. I press for more morphine. One more lick. One more lick to forget that I have no more years. One more, and the morphine lights up my veins. I'm glowing. Machines hum. Real cicadas singing in tall grass, under the tree where my swing hangs.

# LEMON TART

Open wide lemon tart. Zest of orange on the tongue. In the morning: square pastries with poppy seeds. Coffee, dark roast, iced water. And thus, why not slip inside my ear canal. Try it on. Examine the intratubular tunnelling. Vast lands filled with sprouts of cilia. Why not say *something?* And where are the gumdrops? Jar on second shelf from the sink. Glass jar with metal clamps. Always preservation before love. Cookies look good with lemon tarts, but I don't eat that shit anymore. They're for him, fancy pastry tower, floral tablecloth. Are those my cilia rustling with the coffee machine? Singeing cilia boiling water. Dying like little poppy seeds in an oven. Fyodor says they perish with the mixer, but I baked them, so I should know.

Cookies from jar to hand to plate: must be an exhausting sojourn. Remember Paris? Paris was like Cheese Whiz on crackers compared to now: convenient, gooey, carefree. It was as though things would never expire between us. Now heaps and heaps of Bleu d'Auvergne. Unnecessary prestige for such rot.

All our fancy plates love the back of cupboard doors. Kept inside, they can relax. Puffy curtains. French silk. Breakfast nook fireplace was my dream. Only thing: the faucet needs to be fixed. Maybe a swan neck for elegance. A deeper sink for pragmatics. And my pupils must be huge stacking gumdrop cookies on the tier. Gumdrop lemon tart gumdrop lemon tart gumdrop lemon tart and pupils open wide gumdrops.

Before sunrise he doesn't like too much "overzealous overhead lighting," only the repetition of over. But the poppy seeds are so blank this morning. They have nothing to say, blue cheese. The gumdrops are stoic. And meanwhile Fyodor thinks all gumdrops taste the same. Equal flavour, equal synthetics. He thinks children should be taught that red is the same as blue is the same as green gumdrops and we're all one big happy equality.

Myself? I don't think of children. We can't make them. I want only what we can make. Dr. Findleson says we can make a life full of love. But there's nothing fabulous about her. Mediocrity in her leather wingback. Reproduction of her and her husband four times – I saw the family photo on her desk the first visit. Dr. Findleson is on a different polyester planet. No lemon tarts with gumdrop cookies on fancy three-tier pastry towers. No Parisian stained glass in the breakfast nook. She has snot and sticky hands on windows. Wet diapers in the trash. But children are a joy, Fyodor says, they're little hands to wake up for and hold.

Fyodor says a lot of bullshit. My cilia are sound-mills. Bullshit turning them round and round and round, popping neurons in my brain. Yelling doesn't penetrate drum flaps. I imagine Fyodor with a lot of wax in the ears, so I don't say anything back anymore.

Fifteen years together and yesterday my cock was itchy. The clap? Tube of gonorrhea? In Asia they tube yogurt and fish. And my coffee isn't what it used to be, sitting cold. Sitting cold, lemon tart. Wilting. Yes, maybe wilting. Coffee is two hours old after all. I hate when they say "forty years young." Bob and Kelly fawning over my aging body. *Get away, it's gross!* But still. Wake up, gumdrop cookies. Pretty French silk frilly bathrobe. And an itchy crotch. Chlamydia? *No.* Fyodor would never. Fifteen years together, and he would never infidelity. No chlamydia. Chlamydia sounds like clematis, reminds me of Fyodor's mother's vines sprouting out of my cock. Purple flowers. Petite.

Really though: Neiman Marcus fabric softener recommended by Regina Winslow last week. Smells like deep-fried lilac in butterball pastry. Floral and sweet. Sugarcoated and now fabrics are softer, cock-itchier. Its butterball makes ze cock prickly. Or was it you, Fyodor? *No.* Hormone levels are evening out, Dr. Findleson. Enjoy the best years of your life, Dr. Findleson. Fondle your son, Dr. Findleson. But really, why do we pay her? Fortieth birthday and she thinks I want to know my testosterone is plummeting? My sex drive? My desirability?

I'm wilting down below and my cock is acidic. It's all over for us. Mediocrity into the sunset. Isn't the sunset always death? Fyodor and I, a boring retired couple, balding and dry, tinkering at collector trains and scooping cat litter.

So we'll have a baby! – Fyodor's thought. Baby bundle of blubber and burps. Too many B's for me. I see your B and raise you a J. J's are sexier, especially in the lowercase. Let's get a Jaguar instead. Hot baby-girl pink. White leather interior. Maybe a Corvette Barbie car, so you'll get your B, but C's aren't as delicious. C reminds me of Car reminds me of my first boyfriend Carl. Carl, where's-your-tongue? *Carrrrrl,* was your tongue chopped off? *Carrrrrrell!* C is like a big hollow mouth kissing me with no tongue. I like J instead because my cousin Jorge would end all his letters with a lowercase j period. j. So sexy. Jaguar it is.

But Fyodor is determined baby boy. Not girl. Girls are too messy pubescent. Sticky on French satin. Blood doesn't wash out well. Hi Fyodor. Brown eyes look up at me across lemon-tart tower. Too bad, brown eyes. Remind me of big bowls of gravy. Remind me of sitting across from you at Annabella's wedding two years ago. Brass gravy boats and mango chutney saucers.

Gluten-free dinner roll pyramid because wheat constipates Annabella's Raghavendra. Clogs' up his pipes. So we were eating rice pasta and cornmeal cakes when you told me you didn't love me anymore. Then I found you in the bathroom, drunk on Crown Royal. Bowtie drooping. Cigarettes in the toilet. You wanted out because I couldn't give you any of it: Raghavendra and Annabella sticking cake in each other's mouths. Bloating and wedding night sex. Giggly duplicates on the front lawn playing with mud.

I couldn't give it to you.

But later that night it was beautiful on Egyptian cotton. Royal York Hotel. Love. We reconciled. You wanted in. And now: Hi Fyodor, big brown gravy eyes. Hi Fyodor, and you don't even look at me.

You said you didn't mean it back then, drunk fabulous. The Indian music distorted reason. Wild Indipop crackling snap through cheesy strobe lights. My cilia going crazy drug coma.

You look up from the newspaper just now. I open my mouth: No work today. Vincenzo is taking the

Montgomery account, I have the day off… Well, I got up early for you. Brought you lemon tarts and gumdrops… Yes. Well, that's the plan. Lunch with Calista. Tea midday with Giovanni Monterelli about the swimsuit shoot. Plus I want to finish—

I always stop talking when Fyodor stops listening. Fyodor: a man of reason. Just wants the facts from me. Am I working today? – *No.* Do I contribute to this household? – *No.* Am I leeching off him? – *Yes.* This is Fyodor's logic. *Oh, I just want pretty things! Trinkets sparkling! I only work as a fashion consultant for ze perks, ze à la mode and wine parties* – Fyodor can be so nasty sometimes. Meanwhile, he's a stuffy lawyer with brown eyes like impenetrable gravy. Thick, gelatinous, and pupil gratin. Someone overcooked the cheese. Meanwhile, the sun hasn't risen. Fyodor's hum rustles cilia and they don't like it. So bloody annoying.

But look at me, I'm up. Lemon tarts with orangey zang that my noncontributing hands made for him. I ignore his cattiness and hums. Gumdrops are my favourite. Once upon a time, Dr. Findleson said we shouldn't have favourites in our relationship. Celebrate equality. But Dr. Findleson was growing a moustache on her face.

I'm afraid Baby would be a show. Three-tier tower and Jaguars are acceptable, but baby bundles on display, designer baby? Feels wrong. Fyodor never sees it this way. Fyodor says he wants a simple family. A nuclear family. Nuclearosis. Necrosis.

"OK. But Fyodor. Nuclear family doesn't involve me and you. By definition… it just *doesn't*…"

"Why can't it?"

"Well, I don't know, but it's not the definition. It just can't."

"Let's redefine it then? Nino and Ramado are going to be fathers, and Ramado is five years older than us."

"Yeah, and Ramado changed his name from Kevin to sound mucho Italiano. He's also trying to invent nipple inserts… I can't trust anything that guy says anymore…"

Lemon tarts don't remember this conversation, they're too young. But my cilia sound-mills do. They remember the fight afterwards, smashing glass. Glass doesn't smash on its own. Why am I so tired lately? Scratch. Readjust. Imagine teaching a little boy about the "tuck" or the "leg-cross-scratch" or how to dress and look fabulous for tea and biscuits with a lover? High tea never meant on drugs. *Why a father?* Makes me feel like I'm not good enough. Makes me feel: concavity of oesophagus, hunch of shoulders, all the blood leaving my face so my face is a white blanket of nothing and I feel like nothing and I look like nothing and my stomach screams emptiness! emptiness! because anything I put in it becomes nothing. It makes me feel worthless.

Are we almost done here, breakfast morning? How many times have people made a pun on morning? Good mourning, Mr. Hancalapalos, you did a good job mourning. The mourning birds were sad. Meanwhile: My ears are tinnitus. *Ah*! Silly cilia. If I had a daughter I'd name her Cilia Mourning.

"You want what I can't give you… I love you to the moon and beyond – to *Saturn* – but I can never make a baby for you."

"We can adopt?"

"But whose baby would it be?"

One day The Homosexual Man will evolve to grow a uterus. One day a homo-mama. But not now, I'm sorry. And then of course, while I'm staring at Fyodor, it's morning, and I have nothing to do except be a lemon tart unpicked on a plate. Then of course I think of how many heteros have had the same conversation. Woman can't conceive. Or man has no spermoids. And everything has gone to shit because they're supposed to be baby-making machines. How do I deal with stress? Dr. Findleson asks the most ridiculous questions. I stress about my inability to deal with stress. I stress about my stressing over my inabilities to deal with stress. And I've read the articles online. Immunosuppression because I stress and stress and stress. Killing Natural Killers. Kill T-cells. Immune system the lowest. Cancer lovin'. But how to stop?

Lemon tarts don't make things any better. I make them, he never eats them, I feel like crap. But they look so good on the three-tier tower. White enamel ornamentation with soft lemon squares. Poppy seeds sprinkled. I will go to the spa today and spend $1,000. I will feel better about myself lemon tart. Seaweed facial and mud massage. Cancel tea and lunch and enrobe myself, sit in the aquamarine. I'm like a merman in there. Truly. And the silence is comfortable. Not like silence at breakfast table gum-drops. Or me watching Fyodor read the newspaper. Silence breaks while the fast is broken. Silence breaks with inquiry. What will you do today? Quick reply. Then back to silence.

Am I sitting at the breakfast table alone seaweed facial? Am I staring at myself reflecting off the water glass, the three-tier tower, the newspaper crinkling cilia? Your nose hairs were horrifying, but we recti-fied them. Why can't we rectify this? Meanwhile: your laugh sits beside you on the purple chair. Royal and dignified, it laughed for years and years but is now mute. Meanwhile: *Do you still love me?* sits on the counter by the sink. It's been there since 2007.

My voice back then, trembling, my hands washing
the pots, geranium aroma: "Do you still love me?"
Do you still?

# BALLOONS

At twenty-two years, Callie's cysts ate her ovaries, and twisted tubes into malignant spiral staircases. The staircases led to nowhere. They broke apart in places, too dangerous, a looming safety hazard. So we opted for everything removed – wanted it all out, gutted; no hope for remodelling, her reproductive house was haunted, lifeless.

One day in June, with humidity reaching infectious limits, two surgeons cut inside Callie and saw windows smashed, indissoluble dust, antique dolls with heads missing. They used scalpels and antiseptic to tear her walls down. They threw dolls and uterus into formaldehyde dumpsters, pickled some for later analysis. And everything went as expected, perfectly planned. She lost four pounds.

That's how Virgil came into Callie's life three years ago. Callie, so hollowed out and vanished for months upon months, saw either Death or the need to Refill. Coming out of the pharmacy one evening, she spotted a tiny photograph of Virgil on a poster: *RESCUED PUPPIES, FREE TO GOOD HOME*.

She told me his eyes, the deepest brown, seemed just as vacant as she felt. In their loneliness, they needed each other.

Virgil was golden cream, shorthaired. He was soft and playful back then, could fit inside Callie's hollowness and set her free. And months passed with Callie and Virgil in spring meadows. Lollipop tulips, crocuses budding, Virgil wearing the sweater Callie made him; it was white, light cotton, and under the sun that summer he shone.

I'd find them napping out in the cornfield most afternoons. The crickets and cicadas humming, summer sounds knitting into song around them, and everything dry. The world like fragile hay under his fur, her hair, sprawled out together in sleep. Then autumn came, and the world fell away to barren branches, forests of skeleton trees. In all that dark-ness, we worried Callie would fall away too. But everywhere Callie went Virgil went. Everywhere Virgil went, Callie followed. There was no breath for Callie without him. There was no love, no thrill, no reason. And while everything around her perished – that winter so cold it tore to the bone – Callie was beginning again.

Soon months turned into years, and Virgil was three years old. Callie made a cake of buttercream frosting, airy vanilla sponge. There were streamers and balloons and tiny birthday-cake sequins. Everyone came. And Callie, in a white eyelet dress, looked just like an angel, something heavenly, magic. She tied Virgil's navy bowtie delicately around his neck. He sat so still. Snaps of camera shutters, and the two of them captured forever with the fancy birthday hats and confetti. If you look close enough at the photograph, you'll see something fertile in Callie that day, something swelling. Inside her birds were singing their dawn chorus, *Aubade to a Second Chance*. And Callie brimmed with cherry blossoms, devotion, breezy afternoons, lush overgrowth of fireweed and forest. Nature will always reclaim what's lost.

One day, a few weeks after the birthday party, I went with Callie and Virgil to a favourite meadow – it rolled across the southern height of the escarpment, broke at The Peak. We made a picnic of lemon meringue tarts and tuna sandwiches, dog biscuits and carrots, carried it all in a seagrass basket, lay our blanket down. The air was crushingly hot that day. I remember it crept slowly across skin, into pores, boiled over – but they didn't seem to mind. Just play and love, chasing one another, the sunshine and prairie lilies, flights of dandelion dust.

I watched the day unfold from the blanket, a patchwork quilt of sea greens and turquoise. I read

Berryman's *Dream Songs.* Lying on my back, I saw the weeping willow's dancing branches, a mobile above me, heard Callie's laughter in the distance. Then later, midafternoon, Callie and Virgil playing near the horizon, me nibbling on a tart. I looked down briefly to salvage a drip of lemon cream, looked back up – and it was as though an exhaling swoop, a breeze from heaven. I saw the wind blow straight across the meadow and push Virgil over the peak, a golden flicker. I watched his snout to the clouds, the horizon drop – a split second – and the cliff's uncompromising edge. Then I watched as Callie jumped after him, so full she could never float back up.

# So Long,
# Bibbly Bobbly

I was a bat out of hell at seven, riding my bike. Back when the neighbourhood was a country, and tires soared between provinces of sidewalk, regions of driveway. I was on a mission for worms. I was a sun-to-grass interventionist, rode my bike everywhere, determined to save worms from concrete frying. No salt. No pepper. I threw them into shade and mud. I brought them home to my garden, unpacked them under poppies, "Here, *live*, be free."

I never thought about natural courses of existence. It didn't occur to me that some worms are utterly brainless and deserve to dry up, sun-fried, and die. They are the weakest, the lowliest. They deserve death. Back then I saw everything as human invasion: the sidewalk is unnatural. The sidewalk invaded worm-land and forest. We should protect. We should rectify our destruction. I was seven and responsible. I carried the whole country of sidewalk-roadway-worm-death-burden on my bicycle wheels.

I now know the sidewalk is Evolution. It was destined to exist, bound for invention. Just like it was bound to happen that an elderly man swerved to a stop in front of my worm-loving face to tell me I was a bat out of hell. Because I *was* a bat out of hell. I was fast legs cycling and quick fingers saving. I was ruining the course of existence, meddling with Darwinian evolutionary principles of *Die, weakest, die! Die in midday sun slaughter!* For the world, this is hell.

Oh, Mum thought it was cute that I'd save worms and feed them to her peonies – "You're just such a sweet bibbly bobbly, my darling Scottie, you have such a big heart. Keep saving those worms! Keep on keeping on, my darling bibbly bobbly."

Fucking bibbly bobbly. I hated that name. It originated from nowhere, came from some bibbly bib I wore as a child, or maybe the way my fat flabbed jiggly blobbly when I toddled around. Bibbly bobbly seemed a gross misinterpretation of what I was. Mum looked at my worm-saving as some naïve pet project, a seven-year-old phase, a "boy thing." In reality I was a pseudo-Christ. I was playing God and worm-a-teering. When Mum called me bibbly bobbly, all I wanted to do was hurl her on the sidewalk and watch her fry midday. See if she liked it.

My whole childhood I only had compassion for worms. No care for a squirrel hungry on the sidewalk, a badger strewn with his teeth knocked out. I'd ride by, unaffected, into another province, another driveway, my only mission to intervene on worm fries, end sizzling worm death. To campaign for prevention and proaction in Asia where Mum told me they ate worms in soup – *WORMS IN SOUP?* – The pain! I was a wreck for days after she told me, imagining worms moist and chicken-brothed, noodles white, noodles brown, mouths slurping the precious squiggles.

Sweet bibbly bobbly later realized this was a lie Mum told him so he'd hate the neighbours from Taiwan. I still don't get it. She hated that their garden was nicer, their hedge sharper. She hated that Mr. Xiao did everything my dad couldn't do. My dad: riddled with a skin condition that left him bandaged and arrested. Terrifying bubbles. Hard-domed blisters. He couldn't leave the house, couldn't work. All he did was watch *Jeopardy* and change his bandages. *Candid Camera* and change his bandages. *M\*A\*S\*H*, change his bandages.

And sometimes Mr. Xiao would come over to help Mum. He'd prune the backyard trees. Lift heavy boxes. Mum was always pleasant during these moments. Her tightlipped smile, "Thank you, you're such a great help!" Heartfelt goodbyes. Mr. Xiao leaves, then: "That fucking bastard! Look at the mess he left – just look at it!"

At the time I could see nothing except Mr. Xiao filled with worms. His belly-acid frying them to pulpy slime followed by a deep-penetrating colon massage. And all my dreams, brimming with worms like spaghetti entering and exiting his small Asian frame. How could Mum do that to me? Make me hate like that? Her husband was inept. Her husband was a sad pathetic blemish on the couch. So let's hate what's good? Let's teach young bibbly bobbly to fear the worm-eating Xiao? I never forgave her. Partially because I needed something tangible to throw in her face when I finally told her to fuck off. I was eighteen, legally an adult, had enough of her raving lunacy, her goddamn *bibblies* and *bobblies*, so I looked her in the eyes and said, "You ruined my love of Asian culture for years. You exploited my worm innocence. I hate you, you bitch, get the fuck out of my life."

Poor Mum didn't know what to say. Dumbfounded. Shocked. Shocked baby bibbly bobbly would defy her, degrade and relegate Mummy dearest to fuck-off-land. But the truth is, my entire adolescence was spent hating her. I hid it well. Mum had no idea that from the moment I hit puberty onward, all I wanted to do was pinch her dimples and fry her outside in the sun. Or shave her head and wrap Dad's soggy bandages around her scalp. Or fill her with sacrificial worms, see what would happen. Everything I felt was locked up behind acne smiles and rotten teenage breath – and I was angry, so fucking angry, at the state of the world, the comfort of my little existence, my cushiony worm-saving afternoons. And I looked at my dad, vowed never to waste away on a couch like him. And I thought of Mum, never wanted to be her either, her manipulative cheeriness, her using, a user of nice neighbours only trying to help her get by. I re-examined my life, deemed it unfit; decided I needed a change.

For as long as I can remember I couldn't figure out who I was or what to do, how to rectify the cushy inanity of my life. Magazines told me I was too acne-covered. I had a big nose. My skin was too reddish whitish blotchy, hair too greasy. I was malformed and tragically North American. I was told to want perfect formation, my own house, my own plot of land, space – lots of space – clear skin, big eyes, and babies, many babies, to carry on my legacy.

A few months after I told Mum to fuck off, I was an official high school graduate. There was a drought through our region; everyone was sweat and air conditioners. Grass fried. Worms fried. Trees began to wilt and yellow. And the sun was too blazing fire; under its heat my acne skin would singe in a second. So I stayed indoors, researched on my computer all day long. Articles. Studies. Laboratory reports. I was in the heat of my identity crisis: What did I want? Who was "I"? I. That erect son of a bitch: "I." Who was he? Who was *"I"*?

What I knew of "I" was repulsion, big nose disgusting, acne warthog, flaky white Caucasian. Why did I need to have a big nose? And eyes and a mouth like mine – why did I need to have them? Why does anyone need to have anything? So I decided I would evolve. I wanted to progress. To do better than my white roots, my racelessness, my mum and dad suburban scum. And the sidewalk enticed me. The sizzling worm stir-fry. The bat out of hell I used to be! I believed in progress above all. Darwinism. Enlightenment. Human superiority. In the heat of the summer – in the midst of my insane cry for identity – I decided to evolve to the highest degree of perfection: I WOULD BE MR. XIAO.

It wasn't an easy decision. Mr. Xiao is a million genes disparate from me. His facial structure is rounder. Higher cheekbones. Flatter nose. Smaller eyes. And he has a beautifully glowing Taiwanese complexion, thick hands, shiny robust hair. A difficult transformation, sure, but I was determined.

Every day I had an incessant nagging in my stomach, a boisterous itch across my heart: I wanted IN on his Asian-ness. I wanted to be from the Orient, glorious ancient land, mountainous, oceanic. I wanted to know that little island so intensely, NEEDED to go there in my Asian-ness, integrate, establish, leave this blazing suburban inferno behind – my need and want so overwhelming, nothing could stop me.

Money. Money was always my biggest obstacle. I was qualified to nowhere. A greasy high school graduate, lanky as fuck, couldn't survive heavy lifting, would only scare away customers. How could I get enough money to afford anything?

Then, by chance, my dad died. Apparently one of his bubbles popped and his bloodstream filled with disease. What a septic man, maybe I should've felt worse than I did? He was my dad after all, he gave me life. But wasn't it just a fun fuck for him? Wasn't I just the grimy byproduct he ignored most of his life? OK. So my dad died. I was sad. But I was also tickled by fate, happy for the money. Lots of money. Half to Mum, half to me, right in time for my transformation.

Just like the smartest worms, the ones who stay in their muddy palace, I would be the smartest of my kind. I would become Asian. I would BE

Taiwanese, manufactured that way, transformed. How I saw it: Man was always meant to invent facial surgery. Man was meant to evolve and try on different races. Mr. Xiao was the only human being I respected. He was the only human I thought was human and I was often right. Therefore: I would shed my whiteness, my mutt skin. I would evolve.

When I first told the plastic surgeon my plan, she was outraged – "You can't just change races like that! That's completely wrong, politically incorrect – I won't do it. GOODBYE."

But I had my arguments laid out. In Asia they have plastic surgery to look more Caucasian, right? And a lipless woman can inject to lusciousness, right? – I lied and told her I always felt Asian, from my wee years, I identified with Asian men, Asian culture, I would tape my face and skin just to look that way. Then I began to cry. A teenage guy crying is always cause for sympathy. I told her my dad died young. And my mum was a racist. And I had to hide my true identity from both of them my entire life. My youth was full of shame and hurt, and I felt betrayed by everyone around me, including my own body.

With enough tears and persuasion, all people acquiesce. Soon I had a doctor's approval. I was on the road to revolutionary. I was ready to remove my face and put on a new one. Elated. Excited. Ready. Ready for respect, *self*-respect, culture, my Taiwanese homeland, the endless possibilities! All I wanted: to snip-snip into Asian, slip out the back door of Mum's house, into the world, across the ocean, onto my island, marry a sweet Taiwanese woman, love her till the day I die, and be buried in the land where I belonged.

That was the plan.

Of course, plans don't always go as they should. People get in the way. People are pests and accidentally die. But, what I will say is my heart was in it. From day one, my heart was pure, it had the best intentions.

Every part of my surgery went perfectly, followed by months and months of rest, convalescing in my care facility. There were palm trees, ocean tides, breezy Californian afternoons with gauze and painkillers. But I could never be grateful for the beauty – not until I removed my bandages and could be less like my dad and more like Mr. Xiao. I kept telling myself: When I can look in the mirror and see ME, see my Asian-ness shining back at me, then I can be grateful for the world and its creatures.

Luckily my eighteen-year-old body was healthy. It mended and repaired like a worm cleaved in two. That's what I was – a worm split apart, one half healed and following my true destiny, evolving into a separate being better than before. And I finally removed my bandages to reveal beautiful almond eyes, round face, flat nose. My acne was gone too, just scars left behind and concealed by darkly stained skin. I was a Xiao like the world had never seen. A new man. A man ready to live.

Next in my plan: a quick stop at Mum's house. I needed to pack up everything before my exit to Taiwan. Walking there still felt the same. One has a concept of one's "face" – mouth, eyes, nose, chin – but never in detail, only vaguely iconic. I never thought of myself as Asian greeting others, Asian waving, Asian smiling, Asian with tinges of familiarity. I walked Poppy Lane, across the tracks, through the back path and into my country like Scott Wilson did for eighteen years. I kicked the bigger stones like Scott Wilson would do. I waved to neighbours. Read sidewalk-chalk love confessions. Dragged my hand along the fence. I was fresh Asian but forgot what my face looked like. I was Xiao but Scott and both at once.

I saw Mum's garden in the distance, her peonies were falling open, and everything in the world was alive and vibrant – all colours were fresh to me, ready to be articulated, every texture unfolding for my brown eyes. And familiar sensations of Mum's house, my youth, Mr. Xiao coming over to help us. Remembering Dad wasting on the couch. Worm-saving. The country of my neighbourhood. Mum changing Dad's bandages. Pies. Worms. Bicycles. Ah! Life is so strange. Scott Wilson hated all that stagnancy – saw it as irreversible tragedy, de-evolution, the fall of a species – but me, newly *reborn*? – I revelled in it, was grateful, gratitude, love, calm, appreciation.

The front door was unlocked as usual. I walked inside. Mum was in the backyard, her hums soft through the screen door. I went up to my bedroom, sat on my bed, looked at my posters, my papers, Taiwan fading to the back of my mind temporarily. I thought: This is where I came from. I will leave it soon, but THIS is where it all began.

Then Mum's precious humming in the kitchen, screen door slams shut. Maybe she's picking rhubarb? Or fresh flowers? And I could hear her continue down the hall, into the washroom washing her hands. She hummed opening the bathroom door. She hummed walking back into the hallway, below the stairs, gentle Mumsy vibrations.

"Hi Mum," I called down from my bedroom. My body glowing with longing, needing to be close to her, to hug her, to say a proper goodbye.

"Hi, Mum! I'm back. Come upstairs, I'm—"

"Scottie! – Oh, I'll come up to you! Oh my God! Did you enjoy your vacation? I know after Dad's death, I *know*..." her feet humming, hurrying up up up and down the hall towards my door, hand on the knob, "Sweetie, I'm just so happy you're—"

Then shrieks. Terrifying shrieks. Her vase smashes. Her peonies scatter.

"Mum, it's me, Scottie... *bibbly* bobbly... Mum? – I've missed you so much. I didn't realize until right now. I just—"

Suddenly a deluge of shrill gibberish. Messy in and out of coherence and her feet moving backwards towards the stairs.

"Mum, come here, *please* – I *miss* you..."

I stretched out my arms to hug her but she kept moving away from me. She wouldn't stop, just kept going, and going. And those shrill animal noises. And that blank face. Her blank face. Falling.

## Acknowledgements

"Winter Immemorial" is a story inspired by Edna St. Vincent Millay's sonnet "What lips my lips have kissed, and where, and why."

Love and Gratitude to:

Nicholas Papaxanthos, for the endless pie which sustained me through the most dire and tumultuous of seasons; Stuart Ross, who drew me out of my shell and was my first reader, my first mentor; Barry Callaghan, for rescuing me from the slush pile and having faith in me; and Alex Chouinard for being the greatest of friends.

I'm also thankful for the unfailing love and support of my family – without you I wouldn't have survived the last twenty-seven years with so many day-dreams. And especially to Benina Miscione and Janet Fawcett (for their strength), Michael Callaghan & all those at Exile, Allison Chisholm, Michael Casteels, David Florence, Fiona To, Yvonne Garry, Michael Gallant, Jeffery Donaldson, and Sarah Richardson. My cup runneth over.

Finally, a big thank you to the Ontario Arts Council for its generosity towards this publication, Matt

Shaw for his editing wizardry, and any who have read my stories when they were still mere embryonic sketches.

Christine Miscione is a fiction writer, with a recent MA in English Literature from Queen's University. Her work has appeared in the literary journals *ELQ/Exile: The Literary Quarterly*, *This Magazine*, and *The Puritan*. In 2011, she was the recipient of the Hamilton Arts Award for Best Emerging Writer. In 2012, Christine's short story, "Skin, Just," won first place in the Vanderbilt/Exile Short Fiction Competition, emerging writer category.

Find the author at
www.christinemiscione.wordpress.com